FAULT LINES

Stan Leventhal

ℬ
ℬ

BANNED BOOKS
Austin, Texas

A BANNED BOOK

FIRST EDITION

Copyright © 1989
by Stan Leventhal

Published in the United States of America
BANNED BOOK is an imprint of Edward-William Publishing Company
Number 292, P.O. Box 33280, Austin, Texas 78764

ISBN 0-934411-26-3

This book is dedicated to Murray Leventhal, Pearl Leventhal, Gary Leventhal: Father, Mother, Brother.

Chapter 1

When he regained consciousness, Kevin opened his eyes and lifted his head. The first thing he noticed was the dark and then the cold, damp concrete beneath him. His hands were bound behind his back and he lay on his stomach. There was a dull throbbing in his brain and he could feel a sore spot on the back of his head. He wondered where he was, how he'd gotten here, and what had happened. It was like emerging from deep water, gasping for air. Kevin breathed deeply and probed the uncertain corridors of his memory, searching for a sign that might tell him something about his present situation.

The last thing he could recall was kneeling to tie his shoelace. He'd been eating at a restaurant — not too fancy but quite respectable — and had gone to the men's room. On his way back to the table he'd noticed the flip-flopping shoelace. He'd knelt to tighten it and suddenly his senses had shut down. The world, spinning into a cyclone of confusion, disappeared. He'd been hurled into a void with no light, no sound.

Now that he'd been rejuvenated, it took him half a minute to realize that someone must have struck him from behind. The same someone who'd bound him and tossed him into this dungeon. Although curious as to the reason for this — he'd done nothing wrong, to his knowledge — it occurred to him that he should occupy his thoughts with some means of escaping. Perhaps the key to freedom might be tied somehow to the reason for his abduction and incarceration. As his eyes began to discern the vague shapes before him, Kevin rolled onto his side and teetered to a kneeling position. The blurry forms began to assume definite shapes just as he realized that his legs were not bound. He struggled to free his arms, but the bonds were strong and unyielding. As the reality of this situation became increasingly apparent, Kevin could feel his mouth getting dry, his throat constricting. The cold creepiness of panic sent shud-

1

ders through his spine. Is this hell? Could this be the ever-after? Am I dead?

Eventually his reasoning abilities returned. He attempted to rein in his fear. Soon his shuddering began to subside.

Sharing this dark prison with Kevin was another man, bound to a round, metallic pole. He watched and listened as Kevin began to stir, then spoke as Kevin got to his knees. "I thought you were dead. Good morning. Or afternoon or evening, as the case may be. The accommodations are shit and the food's even worse. But at least we're alive. So far."

Kevin turned to look toward the voice. It belonged to a man. More than that he couldn't tell from where he knelt. Rising unsteadily, he stumbled toward the direction of the voice. He almost crashed into the man, then stopped. It was dark, but, squinting, he could discern hair, eyes, a face. "Who're you?"

"Thad." The man grinned. "Thaddeus Heath. And you?"

"Kevin Conover."

"Pleased to make your acquaintance, Mr. Conover. I'd shake your hand but that's not possible. Since you are mobile and I'm tied to this pole, the advantage is all yours. Do you suppose you could walk behind it and back up to me? Maybe we can untie each other's hands."

Kevin looked at the man's face, wondering if he should heed his request. "What am I doing here?" he asked. "I mean, one minute I was tying my shoelace in a restaurant and then all of a sudden I'm a prisoner in a basement somewhere . . . what are *you* doing here?"

Thad's eyebrows tilted upwards. He chuckled. "I'm here because I'm planning to pulverize Jack Corrigan as soon as I can get my hands on him. If you're here for a different reason I'm eager to know what it is."

Kevin shook his head. "I don't know any Jack Corrigan. I don't know anyone in this town. I'm just vacationing. And I was eating at this restaurant and now I'm here and I don't know what the fuck's going on. Who's Jack Corrigan?"

Thad was about to reply when a creaking noise sounded from above. He cocked his head, then fixed his eyes on Kevin's. In a barely audible whisper he said, "Go back to where you were and get down. Don't make a sound and don't move."

Instinctively, Kevin obeyed. He tiptoed about ten feet away from Thad and the pole, got to his knees, and stretched out on his stomach. Closing his eyes, he strained his ears and heard footfalls coming closer. A gruff voice said, "Just checking." Kevin opened one eye to a slit and saw a flashlight beam slicing the darkness.

"We're still here," he heard Thad say with a bemused tone.

"Just checking," the voice repeated.

The light swept away from Kevin's vision and the footsteps receded into silence. The door creaked and closed. Kevin lifted his head. A moment later Thad said, "It's okay now. Come back here and untie me."

As he got to his feet, Kevin began to tremble. He noticed that the throbbing in his head had almost disappeared. Fear had overwhelmed his pain. His heart pounded against his ribcage, his palms became moist. He didn't know what was going on, but whatever it was frightened him. This could only be a joke or something more serious than he'd ever imagined. Nothing in his prior experience could match his present circumstances.

He moved closer to Thad and regarded him with caution. Either Thad or the man with the flashlight was a criminal. But which? What if freeing Thad made things even worse than they already were? Kevin's throat tightened and his tongue tripped as he spoke. "How do I know that I can trust you?"

"What makes you think you can't?" Thad shot back.

"Look," said Kevin, "I don't know what the fuck's going on here. This is a mistake. I shouldn't be here. They must have gotten the wrong guy." He wondered if he should be completely honest, if further harm would come to him if he questioned this stranger. He finally decided that it would be best to take the risk and ask the question that might worsen the situation. "What if I untie you and it turns out that you're a criminal? Or what if I untie you and you won't untie me? Then you could do anything you wanted and I'd be helpless."

Thad laughed. A deep, throaty sound. Shaking his head, he chortled, "Silly boy. Look. I'll untie you first. Then you can decide if you want to try to get out of here by yourself. But I'm telling you — they've got guns. We've got nothing. As far as my being a criminal goes, well, I'm certain Corrigan and his thugs think I am. But I'm telling you, they're the ones who are out to get *us*! Somebody hit you on the head, right?"

"Yes," Kevin admitted.

"And tied you up and dumped you down here, right?"

"Yes."

"Could I possibly have done that and then tied myself up? *Would* I have done that?" asked Thad, exasperated.

3

"I guess not," replied Kevin, a bit confused.

"So, Kevin, pal, walk behind this pole, turn your back to it and let me see if I can untie your hands. Then maybe you'll realize that you should return the favor."

He did as he was asked. His wrists burned as he felt Thad's fingers grappling with the tightly knotted rope. He tried to ignore the pain and focus his attention on the room that held him captive.

He sniffed the air; cool, salt-watery, damp, musty. There were no windows. A sliver of light emanated from the door at the top of a staircase. Cartons and crates were stacked against the walls which rose to a low ceiling. Perched above a work table with jars, cans, and newspapers were three parallel shelves, sagging in the center from the weight of more jars, cans, papers.

Thad clenched his jaw muscles as his fingers — pulled behind him, his arms encircling a cold, hard pole — worked to find a yielding inch of rope. Had the constraints been new and less supple, his task might have been easier. But the knots were as tight as only those of a worn piece of rope could be. Thad's arms had already grown numb from their awkward, trapped position. His exertions awakened the sensations of wearied muscles forced into acute bondage. Just as his fingers would grasp a tight arc and pull, he would lose his grip and silently curse his bad luck.

After several minutes with no success, Thad sighed. "I can't do it. My fingers just won't . . . Could I somehow persuade you to have a go at the knots around *my* wrists?"

Without replying, Kevin instructed his fingers to find a chink in Thad's ropy handcuffs. He backed up a step and felt the pole press into the division of his buttocks. Lifting his heels, rising to his toes to attain a more strategic angle, he sought entry among the mass of tight loops. After vain attempts at several strands, he too ceded defeat.

"No way," he said. "What now?"

"It occurred to me, a couple of days ago — I've been here for almost a week, I think — that there might be something on that work table that could be of some help."

Kevin moved away from the pole, his eyes scanning the table and shelves as he approached. There were no tools, nothing metallic or sharp, but perhaps there was something else that could be useful. He squinted and brought his face closer to the jars. Paint, turpentine, dirty water, various powders, buttons, nuts, bolts, nails, screws. A nail might work, he thought. But as his eyes roved across the shelf above, he spotted a sealed flask labeled HC1. He congratulated himself for paying attention in high school chemistry. "Ah ha," he said triumphantly.

"What's that?" asked Thad.

"Hydrochloric acid."

Kevin turned and hoisted himself to a sitting position on the table. He brought his legs up, maneuvered himself to a kneel, and groped for the flask behind his back. As carefully as he was able, he grasped it with both thumbs and pointers, then slowly sat and delicately eased himself off the table. After returning to his former position behind the pole, he held the flask against Thad's hands and said, "See if you can pull out the stopper."

Thad grasped the top, about the thickness and circumference of a nickel, and pulled with increasing intensity. It made a scratchy glass-on-glass sound as it finally gave way.

"Be careful with that stuff," said Thad.

"I will."

Attempting to spill just a drop on Thad's bonds, Kevin tilted the flask slowly and carefully. As it almost reached the proper angle, he could not move his arms any further. But, desperate to attain his goal, he forced a painful twist of his wrists, which caused several drops of acid to escape. One sizzled on the tip of his right pointer. Kevin gasped and moaned, then dropped the flask, which shattered at his feet. A faint hissing sound drifted up from the floor and an acrid odor rose to his nostrils. At that moment, the door at the top of the stairs opened and an unsteady flashlight beam angled toward them.

It was too late for Kevin to feign unconsciousness. And he could barely conceal the pain of the acid eating into his skin.

A woman's voice said, "Be quiet and follow me. They're all asleep but they'll be up soon. There's a van parked in the garage. I'm not sure where it's headed, but I can sneak you inside. Once it leaves here you're on your own."

The light caught the shattered flask and wispy fumes. The woman's tongue clucked against the roof of her mouth. "I was wondering when you guys would find the acid."

"I burned myself — by accident," Kevin blurted.

"Shsh," she replied.

Wedging the flashlight between her upper arm and torso, she untied Kevin's hands, then Thad's. She led them to the small bathroom on the other side of the basement where Thad

had been allowed to relieve himself two or three times a day. Rinsing his hand beneath the silvery spigot that reflected the flashlight beam up into their eyes, she then dried Kevin's hands on her apron.

"Listen," she said as both Kevin and Thad tried to make out her features, "if the assholes upstairs ever get a'hold of you guys again — don't tell them I helped you. I'll be dead meat. Tell them you used the acid to escape. Okay?"

"No problem," said Thad.

Kevin agreed, "Okay."

They could discern her height, about five feet, five inches, and her slender build. Aside from the earrings dangling by her throat, nothing more could be seen. She moved quickly, kicking the ropes that had bound their wrists into the sizzling puddle of acid by the pole. Putting her fingers to her lips, she shushed them again and lead the way up the stairs, following the weaving beam of yellowish light. They walked down a carpeted corridor with framed pictures on both walls. Then down two steps to a door which separated the house from the garage. "This is the only way out unless you have a master key, which I don't," said the woman.

In the light coming through the windows of the garage they could see her face. About thirty-five-years-old, she looked Mexican; dark skin with big eyes and straight, black hair. She opened the door of the van and waved them inside.

"Remember," she whispered, "you never saw me before."

"Thank you," said Kevin.

Thad said, "Ditto."

"SH!" she replied.

The van had been backed into the garage. They climbed in. She quietly closed the door behind them.

They looked around the small space in the dark of the van. When their eyes adjusted they found stacked boxes of running shoes, a carton of plastic crucifixes, and bundles of pamphlets tied with white string. Kevin and Thad seated themselves on the floor behind the partition separating the driver from the cargo. They leaned their backs against the sides, opposite one another. For the first time they could study one another's features. They stared, expressionless, massaging the blood back into their numbed arms.

They were distracted by the sound of someone raising the garage door. The driver entered the vehicle and gunned the

6

engine. The smell of gasoline seeped through the floor as the van rolled forward.

It stopped, the engine idling in neutral. They heard the sound of the door opening, the garage door closing, and the van door slamming shut. The van turned right and moved down a steeply inclined street, over pavement that had been torn up and patched together, broken and repaired, a cycle that stretched back to the taming of the city, the arrival of populations and businesses. As in all modern cities, everything would repeatedly fall apart and eventually be put back together. A pattern as reliable and endless as birth culminating in death, the revolving set of seasons, and the planet's journey around the flaming sun.

Chapter 2

Jack Corrigan's house, on Vallejo Street, near the peak of Nob Hill, had been built about thirty years after the earthquake of 1906. An Edwardian structure with turrets, towers, and gable windows, it had been renovated internally in 1959, and repainted white outside for the third time in 1962.

Originally occupied by the family of a Swedish textile importer, Corrigan bought the house, a bargain, from the youngest daughter. The rest of the family had moved away or died and she lived there by herself until Corrigan took over the deed in May of 1968. Aside from converting the rumpus room—in front, beneath the living room—to a garage, the house was unchanged except for the sparse, largely undistinguished furnishings Corrigan had installed when he moved in. Twenty years had passed and the house, a mottled gray obscuring the white paint, was almost exactly the same.

Leona Ramirez closed and locked the door to the garage, then stood still, holding her breath, trying to determine if there was any movement in the house. She heard nothing. Wiping her perspiring palms on the faded blue apron around her waist, she headed for the kitchen. As she reached it, she heard footsteps in the front hall and the closing of the front door. A few moments later the van moved past the window. She opened the voile curtains above the sink, watched it disappear into the hills, and silently wished the escapees good fortune.

Occupying herself with the breakfast preparations, she was able to dismiss her fear. If Corrigan or any of his associates found out that she'd released the prisoners, she'd soon meet the dearly departed who'd gone before. But busying herself with cracking eggs, frying bacon, toasting bread, and making coffee kept thoughts such as these away from the front of her mind.

She stepped into the dining room and set three places instead of the usual four, Kurt having taken the van for his weekly

8

trip. After checking to make sure that the salt and pepper shakers were full and that the milk had not soured, Leona returned to the kitchen. The radio on the windowsill played a bouncy tune she'd never heard before. It had a fast dance beat and sweet, celestial voices.

The sound of murmuring filled the dining room and Leona pushed open the swinging door. "Good morning, Mr. Corrigan, Miss Chin, Mr. Walters," she said.

The doughy-faced, pudgy man waved at her as though she were a winged pest. The willowy Asian woman offered a perfunctory, "Morning." The greasy-haired sliver of a man looked at her with disdain and said, "I'm hungry!"

Leona averted her eyes and moved into the kitchen. As she placed cups and saucers, serving platters, and the juice pitcher on the tray, she talked to herself: "One of these days you people are going to get what you deserve. You'll be skewered, disemboweled, ridiculed, punished, reviled, ostracized, and your souls will bleed for your crimes."

She bore the tray into the dining room and set it on the sideboard. Her smile was manufactured, as fake as the plastic flowers sprouting from the centerpiece on the table.

"Did Kurt leave yet?" asked Corrigan.

Leona ignored the question and set steaming cups of coffee before each of the place settings.

"I asked if Kurt left yet," snarled Corrigan, his white complexion starting to redden.

Leona looked at him blankly. She pointed to herself.

"Yes, you, damnit," he barked.

"I no speaka da English good," she said to him, you murderer, she added silently. Turning away, she fetched the egg platter, the toast tray, and the bacon dish.

"Give it up, Jack," said Suzie, "she either won't or can't respond. Every word you say to her is a waste of breath and you ought to know it by now."

Sam greedily loaded his plate and dug into the hill of fluffy scrambled eggs with his fork.

"I think I heard the garage door a few minutes ago," Suzie added. "Kurt must already be on his way."

'These eggs are cold," said Sam. He regarded Leona with a menacing stare.

"In that case," said Corrigan, tucking a napkin under his chin, "why don't you take a trip downstairs and see how our guests are doing."

9

Leona's heart thumped faster and harder.

"Shitfuck!" shouted Sam. He slammed down his fork, slid off of his chair, and headed into the hallway.

"Did you sleep well?" Corrigan asked as he scraped his toast. Suzie looked at him with melting eyes and replied, "Delightfully. You?"

"Like a rock. You'll have to go to the church today. Take the bank deposit. I have a meeting with Joe Harewood. We'll rendezvous later this afternoon."

Sam, hyperventilating, burst into the dining room. "They're gone! Gone!" Corrigan tore the napkin from his chest and flung it at his plate. Standing up, he overturned his coffee cup.

"Come over here and clean this up, Leona," Suzie ordered, moving away from the edge of the table, pointing at the oncoming stream of hot liquid. Leona grabbed a napkin from the sideboard and moved to the table.

"What d'ya mean, 'gone'?" asked Jack.

"Just what I said. They're gone. The ropes are on the floor with broken glass." Sam stroked his mustache, his eyebrows raised in quizzical arcs.

"Damnation!" thundered Corrigan. "What do you know about this, Leona?"

She stopped soaking up the spilled coffee just long enough to fix him with an innocent stare, then walked into the kitchen with the damp napkin. When the door swung behind her, she brought her hand to her mouth and fought to control the nervous giggles that threatened to leap from her throat. She heard the three of them arguing beyond the door as it rocked to a standstill, then poured herself a cup of coffee and sat at the kitchen table, listening to the radio.

Jack Corrigan, Suzie Chin, and Sam Walters hurried down the hallway to the basement door.

"The lock's not broken," said Jack. "Must've been an inside job." He stared at Suzie and Sam like a polecat ready to pounce.

"Unless someone forgot to lock it," said Suzie, looking at Sam accusingly.

"I know I locked it! I'm sure!"

Corrigan shifted his bulk down the stairs one step at a time, the others right behind him. Switching on the light at the foot of the stairs, he looked at the oozing puddle on the floor. "I forgot about the acid," he admitted, pounding his palm with his fist. "But how did they get out of the house? I know all the doors were locked from the inside because I checked them myself before I went to sleep."

"Except for the door to the garage which doesn't lock," said Suzie. "Either they escaped when Kurt opened the garage door or," her eyes lit up with the light of revelation, "they're *in* the van and Kurt doesn't even know."

Corrigan turned and grasped Sam's shoulders. "Take the car and don't forget your gun. See if you can catch Kurt before he reaches Mill Valley."

Sam grumbled, then turned and ran up the stairs.

Corrigan switched off the light and ushered Suzie up the staircase. "What are we going to do?" she asked, looking back over her shoulder. Her straight, black hair swayed so musically when she turned her head.

"Business as usual while I think this thing through."

"Do you want to drive me to the church, or shall I drive you to the bar?"

"I'll drive you," he insisted, "after Leona fixes us some fresh eggs and bacon."

☆ ☆ ☆

By keeping track of left and right turns, uphill climbs and downhill plunges, Thad was able to guess that the van was heading north. And after they'd crossed the Golden Gate Bridge, he was certain. The texture of the roads beneath the wheels was smoother. The curving, sloping highway wasn't like the streets of the city they'd left behind. But the ultimate destination of the vehicle was beyond his certainty. The little he knew about Corrigan was enough to convince Thad that he had to be stopped. But there was a great deal more he'd have to figure out before he knew exactly what was going on.

Thad knew that Corrigan had murdered a politician and was probably swindling gullible people out of their money. And that the money was spent to establish a power base for a band of evil thugs. Apparently the law enforcement agencies were not yet aware of Corrigan's crimes. Thad believed it was up to him to try and bring this to the attention of the proper authorities — and at the same time do whatever he could to foil the plans of Corrigan and his gang.

The van swerved around a tight curve and Thad had to press his back against the side of the van to avoid toppling over. When he attained stability, he looked at Kevin, sitting opposite, wedged between a bundle of pamphlets and a stack of shoeboxes. The kid looked scared. Thad estimated his age

11

to be around twenty-eight. He had sandy hair, striking eyes, and boyish features. A few inches shorter than himself, he had a slender but solid build and wore a striped Beaumont shirt, belted, pleated pants, and a windbreaker.

Thad recalled that he'd said he was on vacation. But where was he from? And he'd claimed no knowledge of Corrigan and his activities. This might be true. Kevin could have been abducted by accident. Corrigan was paranoid enough to suspect anyone of being out to get him. But if someone *does* have enemies, then could he be said to be paranoid, or simply realistic?

Thad's instincts told him that Kevin was just a simple guy, not out to harm anyone. But he decided that caution would be wise and that it was premature to confide in Kevin until he knew more about him. And they couldn't communicate anyway until they'd gotten away from the van. Thad had no idea when that would be or how it would be accomplished. He tried to relax, telling himself he might as well enjoy the ride and save his energy for the first opportunity of escaping.

As the van continued into the foothills north of the city, Kevin was bursting to ask Thad a million questions. Where were they heading? Who was the woman who'd helped them escape? What would happen when the van finally reached its destination? And most of all, who was this Corrigan character who'd knocked him out and tied him up?

He tried to read the title on the top pamphlet of the bundle beside him, but the angle of vision was too awkward and the interior of the van too dark. So Kevin studied the figure sitting before him and tried to decide if the man who'd introduced himself as Thaddeus Heath was friendly or just pretending to be. He had very dark skin and very white teeth. A round face with small ears and short, closely cropped hair. He wore a jogging suit which accentuated his robust frame. Around his neck, something shiny dangled on a chain. Thad appeared to be intelligent, educated, very much under control, and exceedingly polite. It was his cool, assured demeanor that had kept Kevin from sliding into a state of utter panic when he woke up and found himself tied and face down in the dark.

Kevin examined the tips of the finger on his right hand. The pointer still burned a bit in spite of the rinsing, but the damage looked negligible. Kevin had once read a book about a forger who'd altered his fingerprints by burning them away with acid. He wondered if the whorls and swirls of his own trademark would suffer permanent damage from the acid he'd spilled. He hoped not, but there was nothing he could do about it just then, so he tried to think about other things.

Thad watched Kevin examine his fingertips and fixed him with a questioning look. "It's not too bad," Kevin whispered. Then asked, "Where are we going?"

"North."

"How far?"

Thad shrugged.

Kevin patted his stomach with one hand and pointed at his mouth with the other.

Thad whispered, "Me, too."

"How long was I in that basement? Hours? Days?"

"About a day and a half, I think, but I'm not sure."

During the moments of distraction—when he had to deal with the immediate—Kevin was able to forget the questions poised to spring from the contours of his brain to the edge of his tongue. They could be headed for a trap, an ambush. Or, their lives could be snuffed out by the driver as soon as he discovered their presence. Kevin's projections into the future looked bleak.

Thad didn't share these fears. He believed that he knew enough about the situation to handle any unexpected occurrences. The only thing that caused him concern was the young man sitting opposite. Kevin was young, but bright. He seemed honest and reliable. But would he be dependable when nose-to-nose with danger? Could he look without flinching at the lethal end of a loaded gun? Would he panic or remain cool when forced to acknowledge his mortality?

Kevin clenched his jaw and looked down at his feet. He reached around to feel his rear pocket. He noted with relief that his wallet was still there. But his suitcase was still at the guesthouse and his bill was running up. Surely the hosts would be wondering where he was by this time. He realized that the first thing he had to do was call them and let them know that he was all right and would return to claim his belongings and settle his bill as soon as he was able. Then he'd have to call his roommate Bryan back home and let him know about this unexpected adventure, not included on his itinerary.

The van continued onward, at a slower pace now that the road had become even more hilly and curvy with steep inclines and banked turns. Eventually the vehicle slowed to a stop. Thad and Kevin alerted themselves to the possibility that the journey was over. But the van resumed its forward motion a minute later.

"Red light, probably," whispered Thad.

Kevin nodded.

About ten minutes and two red lights later, the van stopped and the engine was turned off.

Chapter 3

Suzie waved goodbye to Corrigan as the car pulled away from the curb. The sun had not yet appeared over the rooftops and the street lay swathed in shadows. Adjusting the shoulder strap of her purse, Suzie—tottering slightly on high heels—walked up the steps leading to The Church of Divine Forgiveness, as the small, wooden sign proclaimed. A three-story Victorian building, it stood away from the street on a lot with patches of brown grass, rocky soil, and taunting weeds. The church looked fairly respectable but the faded paint, bleached shingles, and weathered beams bore witness to the lack of care. It had once been home to the bastard son of an oyster magnate. The building had been kept in beautiful condition until the son, who'd never married, died and it went on the market. Purchased by a real estate shark in 1957, the house was partitioned and rented out as crash pads. A succession of artists, musicians, writers, drug dealers, motorcycle gangs, and religious cults had moved in, then departed. In the early 1980s it was bought by Jack Corrigan. He rented it to Reverend Lawrence Bates, who lived with his family on the second floor. The ground level had been converted into a chapel with a pulpit on a stage and rows of antique pews.

Suzie entered the double doors as the Reverend fulminated at the sparse congregation. She sat toward the rear and watched his performance. He was a tall, slim man with silvery hair and a long, pointed nose. His cheeks were hollow and he wore a billowy black gown. After establishing eye contact with the congregation, he would lift his face and address several remarks to the fake stained glass windows painted on the walls and the large candelabra dangling from the ceiling. As taped organ music played in the background, Reverend Bates wound up his sermon.

". . . and so my friends, you must look into your hearts and especially, you must look into your pasts. Perhaps at some time when you were a child you stepped on an insect. God does not like that. Maybe you stepped on a crack so your mother's back would break. God does not like that either. Or you may be one of the guilty souls who stole candy from the corner store. God does not like that. Which is why he is punishing you. Punishing you for your sins. For we are all sinners in the eyes of God. And how can we make up for the sins of our past? With donations. God needs money to do his good work. And there is never enough money for God's great mission. So I ask you — in the name of God — to reach down into the bottoms of your souls and give. Give! Give God the help he needs to spread his light throughout the dark universe."

The organ music swelled to a deafening roar, then receded to a low hum.

"As the plate is passed among you, I'm going to ask my good friend, Tom, to show you what he is willing to do for the love of God."

A well-tanned, shirtless man stepped up to the stage. He had unkempt, brown hair, a well-defined torso, and held a dagger in his hand. The surface of the blade was dull, but lightbeams darted from the sharp edge. Tom raised the dagger above his head and said, "I am too poor to give money." His voice was thin and feckless. "But we all must give. I sacrifice my blood as proof of my love for God."

He extended his left arm and brought the tip of the dagger to his outstretched forearm, below the crook of the elbow. He stabbed himself and drew the knife several inches. A crevice split open and blood dripped freely, like liquid rubies on a melting bracelet. As the blood soaked into the floorboards of the stage, the congregation gasped, the men reaching into their pockets, the women clicking their purse clasps. As Tom stood there holding out his arm, now streaked with dark red, a boy in a clean white robe appeared with a large collection tray. He wove his way through the pews and accepted their contributions.

Reverend Bates stood with his hands forming a steeple, his eyes staring at the ceiling. Then he looked out over his congregation and noticed Suzie. He nodded to her and gestured with his eyes for her to meet him behind the stage. He disappeared into a black curtain as a huge gong sounded throughout the chapel.

16

As the altar boy approached her, Suzie darted up the aisle and found the break in the curtain at the rear of the stage. In the small room with green walls and moldy looking furniture, she waited as the Reverend bandaged Tom's arm.

"Suzie, my dear," said the Reverend. "I'd like you to meet the newest member of our family — Tom Slater."

He moved toward her and shook her hand. "Nice to meet you, sorry to be so abrupt but I've got to run just now." Grabbing a shirt from the green cushions of a dilapidated love seat, he rushed out of the room.

Suzie regarded the Reverend as though impressed. "That was a new twist. Was it real blood or was it somehow faked?"

The Reverend smiled at her, his thin lips curling over brown teeth. "Quite real. It's his 'thing' as he puts it. And the audiences love it. Really puts the fear of you-know-who into them. They're quite generous whenever Tom makes an appearance."

Suzie's blood felt icy cold, her stomach queasy. She attempted to hide her discomfort. "I hate to be in a rush but I wasn't able to drive over myself and I have to catch a bus to keep an appointment."

"Ah, yes, Mr. Corrigan's fee. Just a moment, please."

Reverend Bates left the room. Suzie wanted to sit down for a moment. Her knees were shaky and her head felt swimmy. But the furniture looked germ-infested so she remained where she stood. The Reverend returned a few minutes later and counted seven hundred and forty-eight dollars into her outstretched palm.

"Give my best to Mr. Corrigan and I'll see you . . ."

"Next week, most likely." A feeling of nausea crept up her throat. "Bye." She thrust the money into her purse and quickly departed, moving up the aisle in the chapel, swallowing deep lungfuls of fresh air outside. She sat on the stoop and pulled her hair from her face. Her forehead was damp. She stared at the buildings across the street and tried to forget the sight of Tom Slater piercing his own skin. She thought of the parks in Paris and the sky in Milan. When she felt stronger, she walked down the hill and waited at the corner for the bus.

☆ ☆ ☆

In close proximity to the part of town called The Tenderloin was a small, dingy bar owned by Jack Corrigan. Christened Sutter's Mill, its clientele consisted largely of people drifting toward or away from the fast sex and lurid thrills that made The Tenderloin so popular. Sutter's Mill was not one of the

17

hottest spots in town, but it operated at a modest profit and Corrigan liked having a public forum in which he could assume command.

The bar stretched along the wall opposite the door. A medium-sized rectangular room, the lights were dim, the music vintage, and the furnishings shabby. A film director scouting for 1950s noirish locations would have been pleased.

The jukebox next to the cigarette machine played Sinatra's "Only the Lonely" as Corrigan ordered his third screwdriver. Joe Harewood, swarthy and a bit overweight, mixed the orange juice and vodka, then brought it to the far end of the bar where Corrigan sat. The bartender/daytime-manager knew that he wanted to talk, but he'd been avoiding it, suspecting his mood to be unpleasant. Setting the glass before him, he reluctantly said, "So, how ya doin' Jack, buddy?"

"Not bad. Not bad. How's business?" Corrigan glanced around the bar as if to point out that there weren't many customers.

Joe bristled. "You can check the books right now if you want to — that is, if you don't trust me."

Corrigan sat upright. "Hey, relax. I was just making conversation. I trust you."

"Sorry. Guess I'm a little jumpy today — bad dreams last night."

Corrigan tasted the fresh drink. "So what's new?" He wiped his lips with the back of his hand.

Joe leaned on his elbows. "Not much. You?"

"You know," Corrigan shook his head and grinned, "everything is going smoothly. But there's been one little wrinkle."

"Oh?" said Joe, very interested.

"Well, you know I had Heath as a *guest*," they both chuckled at the word, "but somehow he managed to escape."

"Escape?"

"Yup. And that's not all." He took a long swig, emptying half of the tumbler. Then he belched. "Yeah, there's this kid — the name's Kevin Conover, something like that — you ever hear of him?"

"Kevin Conover," he repeated the name very slowly. "No, I don't think so. What's he look like?"

"Mid-twenties, dresses like a faggot, you've seen the type. Anyway, he was eavesdropping when I was making an important call the other day, on a pay phone. Luckily it was at Maud's. So I knocked him out and dragged him through the back door.

18

Nobody saw me, I'm sure. Got him back to the house and locked him up with Heath. Next thing I know, they're both gone."

Joe's forehead creased with concern as this news unfolded. "What's the upshot?"

"Upshot is — the nigger's loose and he has that videotape stashed somewhere. We already checked his house and it wasn't there. All we need is for him to turn it over to the cops. And I don't know who the kid's working for. Maybe he's a reporter."

"You don't say."

Corrigan shook his head vigorously, then finished the rest of his drink. A woman with garish makeup on her face and a low-cut, gold lamé dress on her body called out from down the bar. "Hey, Joe! Hit me again!"

He moved to refill her glass.

Corrigan was beginning to feel the effects of the alcohol. He looked over at the woman and focused on her bright orange hair and heavily rouged cheeks. "Hiya, baby," he called and raised his glass, empty except for the shrunken ice cubes. "This one's on me. We're pals, right?"

"Anything you say, pal," she smiled. "This one's on him," she said to Joe.

"I heard. I got ears." He fixed a cocktail for the lady and returned to Corrigan. "Another?"

"Sure."

Just then Suzie entered, making no effort to hide her disgust at the seedy, smelly barroom. She glanced around, wrinkled her nose, and moved over to Corrigan, her heels tapping out a martial beat on the wooden floor.

"Suzie."

"Jack."

She noted that he was already drunk.

"Have a drink, baby?"

"*Somebody* has to drive us home."

"Be that way," he snorted.

Joe came over with Corrigan's drink. He smiled at Suzie's big eyes, clear skin, and he couldn't help noticing her tight, short dress, and her trim, firm figure. "Hi, doll."

"Hello," she said, aloof, as though she were speaking to a hamster.

"Can I get you something to drink?"

"No, thank you," she replied, patient, as though he should go spin his exercise wheel.

19

Corrigan put his arm around her waist. "Come on, baby, sit down and be sociable." She perched on the adjacent stool, her spine straight and her shoulders back. "I've just been telling Joe here about the nigger and the queer running out."

"Keep your voice down," she snapped in a whisper, horrified.

"Relax, baby."

"As soon as you finish this drink, I'm taking you home."

"Pushy chink-bitch."

She slapped his face. A thwack reverberated through the room. "Don't you *ever*," she said, her mouth agape.

"Women," said Corrigan, shaking his head, rubbing his jaw.

"Bitches," added Joe.

"Yeah." They laughed.

Suzie tried to contain her rage. Through clenched teeth she spat, "I'm taking the car home. NOW! Are you coming or not?"

Corrigan looked at his wristwatch. "Me and Joe gotta talk. I'll take a cab."

She slipped off the stool and walked out.

"See you later," Corrigan called to her retreating figure.

Suzie walked to the car, just outside of the bar, got in and started driving. She was angry and chewed her lower lip. The late afternoon sun cast a glaze on the buildings that reminded her of some Renaissance paintings she'd seen in a museum in Venice. She asked herself why she stayed with Corrigan. He treated her well most of the time. But when drunk he became abusive and obnoxious. She didn't particularly respect him. The money, though. Lots of it. And Corrigan could be generous if you were nice to him. If you tolerated his dull lectures and nasty outbursts.

She drove for several blocks, then turned down a steep hill. She made a right, found a curb space, and parked. There was a bar a few feet away called Water Works. Inside were red lights, loud music, and people scattered around, sipping drinks. Against one wall, a slim and sassy-looking young man eyed Suzie up and down. She approached him. "How much for one hour with me?"

The man put his hands in his pockets and said, "I don't do women. Understand? But Jeremy over there," he thumbed at a blond man sitting alone in a booth, "he's ambidextrous."

"Thanks."

She moved away from him and sat down opposite Jeremy. Her eyes swept his nice, honest face, his warm eyes.

"How much for one hour with me?"

"It's negotiable." He leaned forward. "What are you interested in?"

"I'd rather not discuss it here." She lowered her eyes. "I'll pay you anything you want. And I'm not asking for that much."

"Your place or mine?" he asked gently.

"Yours."

"Let's go."

Chapter 4

When they heard the engine rumble to a halt and the front door slam shut, they waited breathlessly to see if the rear door would open. After about a minute of strained nerves and excruciating anticipation, Thad slowly opened the door and stuck his head out. It appeared to be the exact moment that they could leave the van unnoticed, unmolested. He stepped out into the parking lot, blinking. Kevin followed immediately. Thad closed the door quietly and looked around at the small shopping center. There was a supermarket, a natural food store, a gigantic records, tapes and videos emporium, a drugstore, and a dry cleaner.

Suddenly, a car screeched into the parking lot and stopped as though it had struck a brick wall. A slim, greasy-looking man leaped out brandishing a gun. He yelled. A longer-haired man with a mottled complexion — on his way into the supermarket — turned to acknowledge the shout.

Instinctively, Thad grabbed Kevin's arm and said, "Let's run for it." They scooted around the strip of low buildings and headed up a wooded hill just behind the shopping center. As they wound their way around jutting rocks and thick trees, a gunshot rang out. Leaves fell from the treetops and birds scattered, squawking in protest. Thad took the lead, moving with unusual agility for a man his size. Kevin was right behind him, trying to keep his balance on the slippery leaves of the forest floor.

Another gunshot reverberated in their ears as Kevin glanced back to determine the length of the gap between them and their pursuers. He squinted but couldn't see anything dangerous, then hurried to catch up with Thad.

They came upon a waterfall trickling into a downhill stream and followed the water upward along a trodden path through the rocks and trees. Thad spied a cave off to the side and pointed.

22

He and Kevin rushed inside and flattened themselves on the ground, listening.

They heard the snapping of twigs and heavy breathing. "See anything?" one voice shouted.

"No. Keep your voice down," said the other.

The sounds of the hunters diminished as they passed the cave and kept going farther up the hill, deeper into the dense forest.

Thad and Kevin started to breathe easier and sat up, staring at each other.

"What now?" Kevin asked.

"We wait."

"For how long?"

"A while. See if we can hear them coming back this way."

After what seemed like a long time, they ventured from the cave and looked about, their ears cocked to catch any hostile sounds. The descending sun cast slanting beams of light, dappling the incline of the hill. Except for the soft wind gently rustling the treetops, there were no sounds at all. Kevin and Thad started walking.

"Wait a minute," said Kevin. "Where are we going?"

"Back to the city."

"How do we get there?"

"Walk, if we have to. Let's try to find a road and hitch a ride. But let's also try to avoid the shopping center. They could be waiting for us back there."

They walked up the hill, circled it slightly, then headed down, making a jagged path across the thick hillside. On the other side of the elevation the sun was blocked, the forest a labyrinth of shadows, a little eerie. Thad and Kevin swerved around a rock promontory just as a woman's voice exclaimed, "Hi, strangers. You lost? Or you just want to be alone?"

In the darkness they could make out a woman — or was she a girl? — with straight brown hair parted in the middle of her forehead. She wore a long, loose gown; a leather pouch hung from a belt around her waist. "I was just going to make some tea and have a few tokes. You're welcome to join me if you like."

Thad was curious to know what this creature was doing in the forest at nightfall all by herself. Kevin hoped she'd offer something to eat with the tea. They looked at one another, nodded to her, and followed when she turned and started walking. "I'm Weslya," she said, leading them onward. They introduced themselves, then followed her in silence. They arrived at a small, wooden cabin. She opened the door and admitted them. There was a thin mattress on the floor and a small fireplace with a few burning logs providing the only source of light. Except for the flickering shadows, it was dark. When their eyes adjusted they could see shelves along the walls with cooking and gardening utensils, books, variously sized apothecary jars.

Weslya gestured at the mattress and her guests sat cross-legged upon it as she gathered a tea kettle and ceramic mugs.

"What brings you guys into the forest so late, if you don't mind my asking?"

"Well," said Kevin, "these two guys with guns . . ."

Thad shook his head and held up his hand as if to say, "Stop!" Kevin ceased talking and anxiously knitted his long fingers.

"What my friend means," said Thad, trying to think of a more plausible, less incriminating explanation.

"Oh, it doesn't interest me one way or the other," said Weslya, unabashed. "Just thought I'd ask to be polite. No one is going to find you here, that's for sure. I've been living here for years and the number of people who just happened to pass by can be counted on the fingers of one hand."

"You live here in this cabin all year around?" Kevin asked.

"Sure do."

"All by yourself?" asked Thad.

"Yes, I do. Would you guys like some cookies with the tea? I make 'em myself. They're pretty good if you're not a slave to a sweet tooth."

She offered a battered cookie tin with a fleur-de-lis pattern. Kevin forced the lid off and pulled out a triangle of semi-hard dough. He was about to take a bite when a gun fired and a bullet ripped through a plank just above his head.

"If anybody's in there, come out now," shouted a voice from outside.

"Down on the floor," Thad said. "Everyone down flat."

He crawled behind the door and crouched. Kevin and Weslya lay pressed to the plank floor.

"You have ten seconds to come out with your hands raised."

Thad readied himself. Eventually the door creaked open and an arm with a gun appeared. Thad jumped up and tried to grab the gun. It shot a bullet into the fireplace, throwing sparks, scattering cinders. Thad and Sam — the dark-haired, skinny intruder — struggled to take control of the weapon.

24

Kurt—the heavier, long-haired guy—entered and Weslya hurled a handful of tea leaves at his face. It blinded him like a sandstorm. As he howled, Thad kicked Sam against the wall. His head snapped against a wooden beam and he sank to the floor. As Kurt stumbled about, gouging his eyes with his fingers, Thad shouted, "LET'S GO!"

He, Weslya, and Kevin were out the door, running through the dark woods as fast as they could go. Slipping and sliding, they grabbed tree trunks and branches for support. Heading downhill, moving as quickly as the dark, uneven terrain would allow, they made it to the winding highway. Cars rushed by and headlights swerved into view, then disappeared. Scrambling over the embankment of a gulley, then up over the opposite side, they stood by the side of the road with their thumbs held aloft.

Four cars passed by, then a pickup lumbered toward them. It slowed to a standstill about fifteen feet beyond. They rushed over to take advantage of their good fortune.

Weslya climbed into the truck. Thad and Kevin scampered into the trailer. The driver, a bearded, curly-haired man with an enormous belly, fixed Weslya with a jovial grin and asked, "Where ya goin'?"

"As far as you can take us." She almost told him about the men with guns and the shootout in her cabin but decided it would be pointless. Why burden this kind and friendly stranger?

"I'm headed for town—Embarcadero."

"Great," she said, pulled her hair from her shoulders and leaned back. The truck rolled forward and shifted into second gear. It was a winding road, gentle up- and down-hill slopes. A cloudy night with the moon only intermittently visible, the on-coming cars lit up the cab as Weslya talked with the driver. She asked him, after a few minutes of desultory talk, if he'd like to try some of her special stuff.

"Sure," he said, turned to her and winked.

She removed a small velvet pouch from the large leather one dangling from her waist. With admirable dexterity she rolled a toothpick-thin joint and lit it with a wooden matchstick. Holding the smoke deep in her lungs, she passed it to him, saying, "I know it looks like a stingy little bone but this stuff is so powerful you only need two hits. Maybe three if your tolerance is high."

He nodded, as if to say, seeing is believing. After his second toke she smothered the lit end and packed the roach in the velvet pouch. Less than a minute later the driver said, "Lady, you weren't bullshitting." Weslya smiled. He turned on the radio and twisted the dial until he found a Fleetwood Mac tune, then glanced at Weslya, thanked her, and glued his eyes to the windshield.

Thad and Kevin, sprawled in the open trailer, not speaking, not thinking, just feeling the cool air whipping around, watched the stars glimmering through the clouds, wondering where they were going. As the lights in the foothills surrounding the city came into view, Thad said, "Civilization. Just like I pictured it."

They drove over the bridge and into the city traffic. The driver left them on Market Street. They thanked him and stood on the corner.

"What now?" asked Weslya.

"We can't go to my place because it's probably being watched," said Thad.

"We can go to my place," said Kevin, "but we've got to sneak in and be very quiet."

They walked up and down the steeply inclined streets until they arrived at the guesthouse near Polk Street, where Kevin had rented a room on the second floor.

Chapter 5

It was early evening, the sun was down and the shades were closed. Corrigan's house was quiet except for the drip in the downstairs bathroom sink. Leona Ramirez was reading a novel about Jewish immigrants in New York City at the turn of the century. She sat on the couch in the living room, her legs drawn up beneath her, her torso erect. The living room was a comfortable place to read. There was a sturdy lamp with a fluted shade between a damask-covered couch and a leather recliner. Leona usually chose the couch and only sat in this room when no one else was home. She loved to read and travel in her mind to distant places with unusual people and different ideas. But she kept her reading a secret so she could pretend she didn't speak English.

From out of the silence, Leona heard a car door slam and footsteps outside. Then a key jiggled into the lock and the front door swung open. Leona closed the book and slid it beneath the couch. She stepped into her terry cloth bedroom slippers and tiptoed into the vestibule. Corrigan staggered in and held himself up against the wall. His hair was damp and his face sagged.

"Leona! Buenos noches."

"Buenos noches, Señor."

"I'm home!" he announced.

Leona smiled at him. "You want eat?" she asked, pointing at her mouth, chewing air.

"No. No. Where's Suzie?"

Leona threw up her hands. "I no unnerstan."

"Su-zie," he said, trying to enunciate clearly.

Leona shrugged.

He swayed, almost lost his footing, then caught himself. "Forget it." He stumbled to the stairs and, lifting his legs with trepidation, slowly made it to the second floor.

Leona heard the door of his bedroom close, then walked to her own room between the kitchen and the garage. Turning

27

on the light, she closed her door, wishing it had a lock. There was no privacy for her here and she hated that. She lit the white candles in the silver candlestick on the chest of drawers. This and the bed were the sole furnishings; the room didn't even have a window. After turning off the light, she stripped to her panties and bra, sat on her bed and reached for a small amber vial of scented oil. She lay the bottle between her legs on the soft, white bedspread. Wriggling out of her panties, pulling off the bra straps, she tossed her underwear on the floor and opened the vial. Her fingertips massaged the oil into her palms, which brought it to her arms, legs, stomach and breasts. In the lambent candlelight, she looked like a fawn on its back, cleaning its limbs.

She tore open the small envelope of a moist towelette and wiped the oil from her hands, then stretched her arms and legs, twisted her torso and arched her back. She groped for the book beneath her bed — an anthology of Nicaraguan poetry — then lay, stomach-down, reading in the candlelight.

The poems took her back to her childhood in Mexico City. She was poor, scared, hungry. Her parents died when she was a teenager. But she'd married, at eighteen, a young man who'd brought her, legally, to California. His name was Enrique Ramirez. He was handsome, healthy. And ambitious.

He'd started out working as a stockboy in a camera store in the Mission District. Leona took in washing and did some occasional baby-sitting. Eventually, Enrique became a salesman and started getting involved in local politics. And then he'd been murdered, just before he was about to run for Board of Supervisors. The police were certain it was suicide. Leona knew otherwise.

His death left her feeling empty. Useless. Until she started to feel that she had to do something. Fight back. Try and find out why her husband had been killed, who was responsible, and how it had been done, She knew that Enrique had been investigating Corrigan. He'd heard rumors that Corrigan was blackmailing illegal aliens — offering the choices of regular payments for his silence or a quick trip back to Mexico. Leona figured Enrique must have found something that incriminated Corrigan. And that Corrigan suspected Enrique had uncovered his extortion operation.

About ten months after Enrique's death, Leona found out through various friends that Corrigan was looking for a cook and maid. Leona applied and got the job. Evidently Corrigan didn't know that Ramirez was married. And if he did, was unaware that Leona was his widow. She'd considered disguising her name when she applied, but realized that that might lead to awkward complications. It probably never occurred to Corrigan that Leona and Enrique could be related. Now all she needed was the proof that Corrigan was responsible for Enrique's death.

Meanwhile, she took pleasure in annoying Corrigan. She'd burn the toast, pretend she couldn't understand him, starch his underwear, and sabotage phone messages. She felt like a tightrope walker risking a fall with harmless pranks, but at the same time was so diligent about the cooking and cleaning that her employer was willing to overlook a great deal. Moreover, he thought that her lack of familiarity with English would insure his secret projects.

Reading was what fueled Leona's imagination, her dreams, her goals. She believed it was impossible to change the world; but little things could be improved. If people like Jack Corrigan could be stopped somehow, the world would be slightly better for it. She read about the struggles in Third World countries and she imagined herself a guerilla fighter, waging the battle for peace, justice, and freedom in her little corner of the world. One person could sometimes make a difference where entire armies had failed. Leona was a soldier with no political agenda, no government to serve, no officers to follow.

She'd begun to keep a diary—in Spanish—of the evidence, clues, and overheard whisperings that she felt could help to expose Corrigan. At night she'd wait until everyone was asleep, then slide her hand between the mattress and box spring of her bed and pull out the black and white speckled composition book. Then she'd write down any pertinent information she'd gathered or deduced that day. Often there was nothing of significance. But tonight she was eager to write about helping the black guy and the white kid escape from the basement. She couldn't, though, until Suzie, Kurt, and Sam returned. If they were to come home while she was writing it was possible that they might burst into her room to tell her to do something. This was too common an occurrence. She'd finally made the decision to always wear next to nothing when in her room in the hope of embarrassing them into discontinuing these intrusions.

While she waited to make certain that her surreptitious activity would not be interrupted and therefore discovered, she read and stretched, massaged her skin and muscles, thinking about the sweet taste of revenge that would someday be hers to savor.

☆ ☆ ☆

The air was so still, the night so quiet it seemed that something must shatter the repose. But all was tranquil as Kevin led Thad and Weslya up the steps to the guesthouse, with Queen Anne towers and floral motifs. The bay windows were dark and nothing stirred. Kevin inserted the key and turned it; the tumblers sounded like bowling pins colliding as they rotated and fell. Kevin opened the door and stuck his head inside. He looked to the right and to the left. Holding his finger to his lips, he waved Thad and Weslya inside, then quietly closed and locked the door. They tiptoed up the carpeted staircase. At the first landing, Kevin turned and headed for his room at the end of the hall. His companions followed. A small nightlight offered guidance.

At the opposite end of the hall a door opened suddenly and a rotund, middle-aged man in a knee-length red nightie burst into the hallway.

"Hello, Kevin. Lovely night, eh?" He smiled at Thad and Weslya. Kevin introduced them to Charles — he'd forgotten the last name — a tourist from Minneapolis, staying in the room next door to Kevin's. "These are some new friends of mine," he hastily explained, adding, "Um, they got locked out of their apartment so they're spending the night here."

"Of course," said Charles, in a tone suggesting that he did not believe this tale but approved anyway. Passing Kevin and heading into the bathroom, he playfully punched Kevin's arm and whispered, "You devil."

The bathroom door closed as Kevin ushered his guests into the room. He turned on the light. Whispering, he said, "Weslya, you take the bed. We'll sleep on the floor."

She was too tired to insist otherwise. Besides, there were more pressing concerns. "Gotta use the bathroom first."

"Me too," said Thad.

"Me three," said Kevin.

They waited in the tastefully, but sparsely furnished room and took turns in the bathroom. Kevin removed two blankets from the bed and handed one to Thad. They used folded sweaters for pillows and got comfortable on the floor after Kevin switched off the light. Weslya drew the bedspread up, punched the pillow, and settled into the firm mattress. In a matter of seconds all three were sleeping soundly, their distinctly differ-

30

ent breathy snores a strange fugue dancing about the darkened room.

☆ ☆ ☆

Jeremy brought Suzie to his tiny apartment, cluttered with newspapers, magazines, books, and files. There was a curtained window, a small refrigerator, a typewriter on the floor, and a bed with a fluffy orange comforter.

"Would you like something to drink?" Jeremy asked.

"No, thank you . . . let's begin." She reached into her purse and counted out fifty dollars. "Enough?"

Jeremy took it, counted, and replied, "Yes."

She took off her clothes and told him to put them on. Naked, she looked skinny and angular. Her clothing didn't quite fit Jeremy and he looked silly, like he was going to a Halloween party. In a wig, makeup, and properly tailored clothing, he might have passed for a real woman. But in Suzie's bra, panties, sheer blouse, tight skirt, and paisley neckerchief, he looked more comical than glamorous. Suzie laughed at him and then called him names: slut, whore, tramp, wanton, fuckdummy, plaything, hustler-meat, and scumbag. She made him march around the room—hup! two, three, four—then stand on one foot until it hurt.

"Does it hurt yet?" she asked eventually.

"No."

A few minutes later. "Does it hurt yet?"

"Yes," he lied.

"Good."

After that she told him to lick her toes. Then she commanded him to strip and she got dressed. When she was fully clothed and he was vulnerable naked, she told him to jerk himself off. She watched, wide-eyed, as his body shook, his eyes closed, and his mouth opened in ecstasy. She then instructed him to wash his hands and gave him permission to don a bathrobe. She lit a cigarette and watched. He tried to ease the air between them with small talk.

"Where are you from?"

"Paris."

"Are there a lot of Chinese people in France?" he asked, sitting on the bed.

"I'm not Chinese," she shot back. "My parents were from Thailand. I was born in Paris and we moved here when I was six."

31

"Oh."

Suzie dinched the cigarette on top of an empty Pepsi can and pulled a twenty from her purse. Jeremy thanked her for the tip. She left his room and walked to the car.

Driving home, she thought about what she'd just done. It had felt very satisfying. She hadn't had an orgasm, hadn't even been touched but she felt content. Hustlers were convenient and money was nice. She'd never done anything quite like this before. Would she do it again? Something to think about.

When she arrived home, she parked the car, noted that the van was back in the garage and that Kurt, Sam, and Leona were asleep. Then she crept into bed beside Corrigan, slumbering like a big, white bear on Seconal. She lay there, listening to him breathing and finally drifted into a colorfully surreal dreamscape.

Leona, who'd only pretended to be asleep — as she had when Kurt and Sam had returned — listened for the sound of Suzie getting into bed. Then she lit a candle and got out her composition book. With a serious expression on her face, she carefully chose each word as she wrote down everything she knew about and could recall that had happened that day.

About an hour after she'd begun, she closed the book, blew out the candle, and lulled herself to sleep with an old melody that strayed into her mind.

Chapter 6

Streamers of light flew from the partially opened Venetian blinds, striping the walls and floor with pale yellow. Weslya, still asleep, babbled incoherently on the bed as Kevin and Thad awoke. Thad was eager to go back to his own house, change his clothes, see if anything had been tampered with. Kevin was hungry and craved needles of hot water bombarding his flesh. But he had his guests to consider. Breakfast would have to come first. He signaled for Thad to follow him and they quietly left the room.

When they got to the bottom of the stairs, Gerrold, one of the guesthouse owners, came in through the front door carrying a toolbox. He had a medium build, thick, curly hair, and a neat mustache. Kevin stopped abruptly. His nerves fired synaptic explosions. According to the house rules, patrons could only have one guest at a time. He wondered if his transgression would be detected and what the penalty might be. Gerrold smiled at Kevin and he nervously smiled back.

"Kevin. Lovely day. Good morning." He held his hand out to Thad. "Gerrold Davis, house mother, glad to meet you."

"Thaddeus Heath," he responded, shaking vigorously, "just visiting."

"I see you're enjoying our city," said Gerrold to Kevin.

"Yes. It's, um, full of surprises," he replied, attempting to conceal his agitation.

"That it is." Gerrold hoisted the toolbox. "There's a leaky faucet on the third floor. Got to run. Have a nice day, gentlemen." He bounded up the stairs.

Kevin and Thad left the building and walked to the bakery down the street. Kevin ordered three coffees to go with assorted muffins, croissants, and doughnuts. As they walked back up the street, they were intercepted by a poorly dressed, heavyset man jiggling a styrofoam cup of coins.

Thad looked at him contemptuously. "Out my face, bro."

Kevin halted, then reached into his pocket for whatever change was there. He dropped several coins into the cup and said, "Nice day." The man thanked him and wished him well.

They continued walking. Kevin shifted the bag of breakfast goodies from his left arm to his right.

"Why did you give that nigger money?" Thad blurted, angrily.

Kevin stopped and glared at him. "In the first place, I don't like the word nigger. I realize that it's politically correct for one black person to use that term when referring to another black person. But still, I don't like it. In the second place, I believe in helping those who are less fortunate than myself." Kevin stared at Thad with triumph in his eyes. He resumed walking.

Thad grabbed his arm. "Whoa, wait a minute, friend. What gives you the right to be so damned self-righteous? What do you mean, it's politically correct? That's bullshit! Because you, the all-powerful white man says so? Let me tell you something about the word nigger. A nigger can be any color, any race, any religion, any sex. A nigger is the kind of worthless trash who makes the world a cesspool. All the time I see all kinds of niggers. But the ones who really annoy the shit out of me are the black ones. I take personal umbrage because they make the rest of us look bad. And I will not support their alcoholism or their drug addictions. And you shouldn't either."

"But something's got to be done about the homeless," protested Kevin.

"That guy," said Thad, "looks like he's able-bodied and he's not a moron, so he should be working, not begging. An easy target for racists and bigots."

"I know what you mean," Kevin nodded. "When I see gay guys that piss me off—because they're acting obnoxious in public or something—or when it's St. Patrick's Day in New York and lots of Irish kids are getting drunk and rowdy all over the place I get angry and I feel like . . . they're making it tougher for the rest of us."

Having reached this understanding, they continued up the sidewalk, entered the guesthouse, and encountered no one on their way up to Kevin's room.

Weslya stood by the open window, facing the mist-frosted foothills. Her arms were raised in a leonine stretch with her head thrown back. Her hair looked wild and free. She whirled around when she heard them enter. "Good morning."

"Good morning," said Thad.

"Coffee and pastries," said Kevin, holding the bag aloft.

"Yum!" she said, waiting for an explanation of the occurrences on the night before.

They sat in a circle on the Navajo rug. With small packets of sugar, tiny containers of milk, and plastic stirrers they prepared their coffee, then munched and sipped.

Between mouthfuls, Kevin explained to Weslya that he was from New York, on vacation, and had been bopped on the head for no apparent reason. Thad took over, explained that he'd been abducted while jogging one afternoon because he had proof of Corrigan's criminality. "You see," he said, "I used to work at Sutter's Mill, the bar that Corrigan owns, and I got wind of the fact that he was setting up some politicians for bad news. When my brother died, he left me a lot of money so I was able to quit bartending. And I asked myself what I wanted to do first and the answer was easy — expose Corrigan for the low-life scum that he is."

Weslya licked some powdered sugar from her lips. "This is so exciting. I haven't had this much fun since I went to a Merry Prankster's party way back when: Hell's Angels, electric Kool-Aid, the Grateful Dead, the works."

"Sorry about the damage to your cabin," said Thad, "and this may seem like fun to you but I think we're in a lot of danger."

"I don't mind about the cabin," she replied. "And I didn't mean to imply that your problems were not to be taken seriously. It's just that my life has been so quiet for so long, I'm just loving this adventure . . . anyway, what do we do now?" She finished her coffee and wiped her mouth with the back of her hand.

Kevin put down his coffee and listened with rapt intensity.

"Well," said Thad, "the first problem is getting into my house. They probably searched it while I was being held prisoner and I have to see if they found what they were looking for. Most likely they didn't or I'd be dead by now. The only thing is they're probably having my house watched so I can't go there myself because they'll recognize me and might try to kill me. Same with Kevin here. They know what he looks like and they think he's with me."

"I *am* with you."

"What about your vacation?"

"It was pretty dull until I woke up in Corrigan's basement. Besides, Corrigan's going to pay for what he did to me. If I can help you get him behind bars, then I'll consider us even."

"And you," Thad said to Weslya, "we can get you a ride back to your cabin."

"Like hell! I want to help you guys and I have a score to settle too. Add bullet holes in my cabin to the list of this guy's crimes."

Thad's eyes narrowed and his nostrils quivered. "This could get dangerous, you know." He looked at Weslya, then at Kevin, determined to convince them of the gravity of this undertaking and also to absolve himself of any responsibility. Another part of him, though, would have done anything to make them join him.

"Count me in," said Kevin.

"Me, too," chimed Weslya.

"Good," said Thad, relieved that this wasn't going to be a solo mission. "I have a little plan to get us to the next square of our deadly game. Kevin, have you got some paper and a pencil?"

"Coming right up." He got to his feet, fumbled in the drawer of the writing desk, and returned to the rug on the floor.

Thad started sketching a floor plan of his house. "Look at this, both of you."

Weslya and Kevin craned their necks, watching Thad's hand make diagrams with circles and arrows on the guesthouse stationery.

☆ ☆ ☆

During the weekday afternoons, between the hours of two and six, there were few visitors to the Church of Divine Forgiveness. With the noon Mass over and the evening Mass yet to commence, worshipers had to do without stirring sermons and breathtaking theatricals. A screen would descend from above the stage and videotapes of tragic disasters — earthquakes, floods, hurricanes, fires, illuminated the darkened chapel. Cameras panned over ruins, rubble, and the survivors' faces. Interspersed were special loops of hands placing donations on collection trays. Maudlin organ music accompanied the visuals.

Above the chapel were two additional floors. The uppermost had a tiny guestroom and attic space. The middle floor had two bedrooms with a living room in-between. Reverend

Lawrence Bates and his wife, Rosemary, slept on a round bed with satin sheets in the room with scarlet drapes to the left of the staircase. Their son, Billy, aged nine, slept in the room to the right, ordinarily littered with toys, stuffed animals, comic books, candy wrappers, and empty soda cans. The room in the center had the color television, dual VCRs, stereo system with CD player, barcalounger, bookshelves, and a long, overstuffed couch.

A subtle, pervasive gloom had settled into the woodwork and fabric of these rooms. Previous tenants, long gone, left traces of their losses and disappointments like the dank, musty odors embedded in an unclean carpet. Whether these vapors, this somber lingering mist, poisoned the present occupants or not is beyond certainty. Perhaps the Reverend and his family brought their own melancholy aura with them. Who can say how much of life is inherited, how much created? The Bates family, whether heirs to misfortune or the source of their own pain, lived in cheerless rooms where the only laughter came from the television set. Most afternoons, the family gathered around this electronic deity, their only connection to other realities. The cathode rays were like tablets from heaven.

Reverend Bates, as usual, sprawled in the barcalounger, dividing his attention between magazines and the television set. His wife, Rosemary, listened to the audio track, staring at her fingernails, painting them a new shade called Tutti Frutti Sherbet. Billy, their son, ate red licorice and commandeered the remote control unit. At every commercial break he'd click from channel to channel, sampling the programs he was missing and other commercial breaks.

Midway through *General Hospital*, Tom Slater poked his head into the living room. "I'm back now, Reverend. I'll be upstairs until the six o'clock show."

Bates looked up from his magazine. "Fine, Tom. See you later." Tom nodded to the wife and child, then headed upstairs to his room. Rosemary blew on her nails, holding them up to admire the color. She had blonde hair stiffly piled on her head, big, brown eyes, and moist lips. Her complexion was smooth and clear, her face round and puffy. "You know, Larry," she said, "I wonder if we're using Tom a bit too often. The novelty is bound to wear off."

The Reverend laid the magazine in his lap. "Until we find someone with more drawing power, he'll have to do."

"Maybe we can find someone who speaks in tongues — or at least pretends to or something like that."

He shook his head. "Old hat. Done to death. We'd have to come up with something really sensational if Tom ever left us. We'll just have to make sure he feels good and comfortable."

She closed the bottle of nail polish and blew at her fingertips. "Well, honey, I still think we should use him sparingly so we don't spoil . . ."

"Stop!" he interrupted. "I'll decide about these things. You worry about your concerns and leave the rest to me. Understood?"

Rosemary looked away and sighed.

"Understood?" he thundered.

"Yes," she said meekly, rose, shaking her fingers, and walked out of the room.

Entering the bathroom, she turned on the light and locked the door. After making certain her nails were dry, she raised her housedress and stuck her fingers between the top of her stockings and her fleshy thigh. Extracting a small foil packet, she unfolded it and dipped her pinky fingernail into the fine, white powder. After four snorts — two in each nostril — she folded the packet and tucked it back into its hiding place. She licked her finger and checked the mirror for signs of powder on her nose, then returned to the living room and sat.

Billy was opening another pack of strawberry swizzlers.

"Billy!" barked Rosemary. "Haven't you had enough candy for one afternoon? Think of your teeth and the dental bills." She swallowed the cocaine drip at the back of her throat.

"Leave the kid alone," said the Reverend from behind his magazine. A nurse slammed a door on the television set, the picture faded, then segued into a wine cooler commercial.

"He eats too much candy."

"I want him to have all the things I never had as a child," said the Reverend as though these words would end the conversation.

"Even the cavities?"

"Shut up. Don't question my authority in front of the child."

"Don't you tell me to shut up," she said, rising to her feet.

"I'll do whatever I please in my own house." He stood up, his forehead pleated, his mouth tight.

"It's my house too."

"THAT'S ENOUGH!" he shouted and smacked her cheek.

Her hand flew to her face, tears trickled from the corners of her eyes. "What did you do that for?"

"This is my house and I'll run it any way I please," he said,

Billy said, "Sh! Dad. It's getting good." His eyes were trained on the television screen.

"And don't you tell me to shush." He strode over to Billy and slapped his cheek. "That'll learn you."

The boy winced and looked up at his father, amazed, confounded. "You both sicken me," said the Reverend. He stormed out of the room and slammed the bedroom door behind him.

Rosemary knelt by Billy's side. She mussed his wispy blond hair and kissed his cheeks. "It's all right," she cooed. "Your father's under a lot of pressure these days. Everything is going to be wonderful soon. You'll see."

Chapter 7

Clutching a tumbler of iced vodka, Jack Corrigan leaned back in the soft easy chair. He'd assembled his staff for a meeting. His intention was to address them in a stern, patriarchal manner. But the vodka softened him, sheathed the edges of his attitude. He was content, avuncular, like a big, white teddy bear.

"Friends, we've got our work cut out for us." He paused dramatically, fixing his gaze on each face. Kurt was afraid he would be reprimanded or possibly fired for letting the captives escape. Sam was eager to secure permission to kill the lousy bastards. Suzie was beginning to wonder how much longer she could hang around with a man who was obviously turning into an alcoholic and cared less for her than he did for wild schemes.

"Kurt, did you deliver the running shoes, the pamphlets, and the crucifixes?"

"Yes, sir. I had no idea those guys were in the back of the van. They were as quiet as mice. If I'd only known . . ." he said, like a fawning nephew, eager to please.

"Don't worry about it," said Corrigan. "We can't be held responsible for our ignorance, can we?"

"No, sir," he replied sheepishly.

"You don't mind me calling you ignorant?"

"No, sir. Not if it's true."

Corrigan laughed. "Oh, Kurt, you slay me. Do you foresee any problems with the running shoes connection?"

"As long as the guy needs powder and you're willing to supply him, we can get all the stuff we can handle."

"And does Reverend Penobscot have a definite date for the opening of his church?"

"Not yet."

Corrigan drained the vodka and walked to the liquor cabinet. After replenishing his glass he returned to the chair and plopped.

40

"How's your head, Sam?"

Sam reached around to the back of his head and felt the bump where he'd connected with the wall of the cabin. "I can live with it. But when do we get to execute those guys? I'm itchin' for action and they're wasting too much of our time."

"Relax. When it's time. First we have to get our hands on Heath's video tape. As soon as this meeting is over, you and Kurt will drive to his house, keep a low profile, and watch for him to return. He's bound to show up there. Once he does, the two of you are to follow him until he leads us to what we want. He'd be a fool to keep the tape at his house — and we know he's no fool. As soon as we have the tape, he's yours. But I think we should hold off with the white kid. He may be a cop or a reporter or something."

Sam looked down at the floor, twisted his neck to work out a kink, then sipped beer from a can.

"Suzie, my dear," said Corrigan. "You got the money from the Reverend?"

"Yes," she looked away, bored, then lit a cigarette.

"And you deposited it in the account?"

"Yes."

"How much?"

"Oh, I can't remember exactly. About seven hundred I think."

Corrigan slammed his glass onto the table. "When I ask you how much I want to know how much!" He glared at her.

She simply stared at him, aloof, mocking.

"And while we're on the subject, where were you when I got home last night?" Suzie looked at Kurt and Sam to indicate that a bit of privacy would be in order for this particular subject. She inhaled two huge lungfuls of smoke. "I paid a visit to my sick aunt."

"The truth!" said Corrigan, his face turning purple.

"None of your goddamn business."

"Kurt, Sam, you can go now. Directly to Heath's."

They left the room, glad to miss this spat. On their way to the door they passed Leona in the hall. She pretended she was dusting the picture frames. When they were gone she listened to Corrigan and Suzie yell at each other for a few seconds, then realized that this would be a good time for her to do a little research among Corrigan's papers. When the shouting stopped, she would cease and protect her ruse.

Dusting the bannister as she walked up the carpeted stairs, Leona listened to the squabble going on in the living room and laughed to herself. She should find another man and he should stop drinking. Those two are poison for one another, she told herself.

She entered the master bedroom and sat at the desk with its stained blotter, antique inkwell, and Rolodex. There were two deep drawers on the right containing files. Leona started flipping through them and stopped when she came to one labeled "Donation Letters." She pulled them out and started reading.

With an ear trained on the ruckus coming from below, Leona attempted to digest the contents of the file as quickly as she could. She discovered that a lot of people had given Corrigan money orders and personal checks to be used for various special interests. There was one letter about setting up a fund to support a right-to-bear-arms lobbyist in Washington. Another to establish a township in Northern California that would only allow white Christians to live there. Still another advocating the legalization of cock-fighting and one to support politicians against space exploration.

Leona, stunned at first, did not understand. But she pressed on. There was a letter pleading for laws against hand guns. And then one right after the other, a letter denouncing U.S. military involvement in Nicaragua and one, just the opposite, in support of U.S. military involvement in El Salvador. Each letter had been sent with a donation. The smallest was ten dollars. The largest, ten thousand.

Leona returned the letters to the file. She flipped through the stiff manila folders, passing one that said "Bar Accounts," and another that said "Church Accounts," until she came to one marked "Donation Replies." It contained carbon copies of typed letters. There was one addressed to the right-to-bear-arms person which stated that Corrigan was in full support of this legislation and had set up a special lobbying fund for implementation. And there were similar letters in which he proclaimed his interest in all-white, Christian cities, civil rights for blacks, the legalization of cock-fighting, the protection of animal rights, space exploration, no military support for Nicaragua, and strong military support in El Salvador.

Then Leona heard the front door slam. She quickly placed the papers in the file and closed the drawer. Pretending to dust the top of the bureau on the other side of the room, she listened intently. Not a sound. She walked out of the room and went downstairs. As she passed the living room, Corrigan called out to her: "Juanita!"

She paid no attention and kept walking toward the kitchen.

"Damnit!" said Corrigan to no one. He struggled to his feet, wobbled for a moment, then plunged into the hallway. "Juanita!"

He came up behind Leona and grabbed her arm, whirling her around. "Didn't you hear me calling you?"

She faced him, affecting the most helpless expression she could manage. "Juanita, I want you to . . ."

"Excuse por favor. My name Leona." She said it slowly and smiled.

"Just a joke. Can't you Mexicans take a joke? Leona, I want you to prepare something special for dinner tonight, something . . ."

"I no unnerstan."

"Dinner!" he roared.

"Dinner. Sí, señor, I cook dinner. Chicken and rice."

"No! I want something special, something exotic and expensive and . . ."

"Sí, señor. No rice. Just chicken. I cook."

She smiled, curtsied, and continued into the kitchen.

Corrigan looked at the ceiling and asked, "Why me, Lord?" Then he pounded the wall with his fist, returned to the living room, and fixed himself another vodka on ice.

The alcohol could dull the sharpness, but it couldn't dispel the images that taunted his memory. As far back as he could remember, he'd been a victim of bad luck. His father had beaten him badly with leather belts, wooden hangers, brass buckles. And he'd absorb the pain stoically, thinking of ways to escape his tormentor and how he'd get his revenge. Other little boys had nice fathers who took them to football games and taught them how to pitch. But Jack Corrigan's father was hardly ever there. And when he was, he'd punish his son for no apparent reason. Mom would just stand by, biting her knuckles.

He ran away from home during his last year of high school. Found a job as a messenger and a bodyguard, working for a numbers Czar. When the racket was busted by the cops, Corrigan managed to escape with a box of large bills. He began to implement various extortion schemes because it was obvious that there were a lot of stupid, gullible people in the world and it would be foolish to ignore such a lucrative market. And those who were weak or vulnerable would and should bow to the demands of the stronger, the more fit, the best suited for survival. This was the world in which he functioned well and felt most comfortable.

After a few more shots of vodka, he stretched out on the couch and drifted into a heavy, dreamless sleep.

☆ ☆ ☆

Kurt sat behind the steering wheel of the red Toyota parked at the curb. His blond hair, askew from the breeze through the window, didn't hide the ears which stuck out like wings. Sam sat in the passenger's seat, cracking his knuckles, fidgeting, singing along with a Motley Crue cassette. They were parked down the street from Thaddeus Heath's house, watching, waiting, slowly growing bored and restless.

When the tape ended, Sam turned off the portable cassette player. "I want to hear side two," said Kurt.

"Do you always get what you want?" Sam sneered.

"Hardly," he replied, drumming on his thighs with his fingers. Sam fancied himself a tough dude. He was Corrigan's right-hand man because he was the meanest, roughest stud on the West Coast. And today, he might have a chance to prove it. When Corrigan's enemies turned up, the negro and the queer, he'd beat them silly. Though he was hungry, Sam ignored the rumbling in his stomach. If there was a job to be done, food could wait.

At twenty-five years of age, Sam felt that he'd finally reached the big time. He'd started out as a member of the Cobras, a gang in Los Angeles. After proving his mettle in one skirmish after another, he'd finally been forced to challenge Ted, the gang leader. The confrontation took place on a deserted stretch of sand near Huntington Beach. Ted was bigger and more experienced; Sam was wiry and more ruthless. They'd begun with fists, but after Sam flung sand at Ted's face, the knives appeared. Sam managed to stab Ted's upper right arm. It was a long slash from the shoulder almost to the elbow. Ted's T-shirt and the sand beneath his boots soaked up the pints of warm, red blood. As Sam stood there all tensed up, his legs planted firmly, ready to carve Ted like a turkey until he admitted defeat, Ted turned and ran, disappearing over the dunes. Sam folded up his blade and looked around at the circle of young men, his eyes establishing his dominance over this gang and this turf. Several years later Sam himself was challenged by a young recruit named Brandon. Guns were the chosen weapons this time and Sam barely escaped, his left thigh ripped open by a closely fired bullet. After making his way north, he lived on the streets for a while, selling fake marijuana, boosting whatever he could. Now that he was Corrigan's next-in-command, he'd found his niche.

It was early afternoon and the morning mists had cleared. The air was warm, the sun bright, as Weslya walked up the steps to Heath's house. Kurt nudged Sam. They trained their eyes on the dwelling and the visitor. She was about five feet, six inches tall with brown hair that hung to her waist. Slender and willowy, she wore a loose dress and sandals.

"She looks familiar," said Sam.

Kurt took another look. "Not to me."

"Where have I seen her before?"

"Beats me."

She entered the house, closing the door behind her.

"I wonder what she's doing here?" said Kurt. "Jack didn't say anything about a girl. He only told us to look out for those other two."

"Maybe we should grab her," said Sam.

"I don't think so. Jack didn't say anything about a girl."

"Then we should follow her. Maybe she'll lead us right to them," said Sam, proud of himself for thinking of this.

They sat there waiting. Sam glanced at the Toyota logo on the dash and shook his head. Someday he'd be in a car from France, Italy or Germany. England, maybe. In time, he'd have more money than he could count and he'd be the master of Corrigan's fortune. It was only natural that someday Sam would topple Corrigan, assume his place and enjoy the power and riches until someone came along who'd force him to give them up.

Chapter 8

Thaddeus Heath lived in a modernized Italianate house, two stories, the exterior painted three shades of blue. There was a small, well-kept yard with grass and flower beds. Weslya thought it looked dreamily charming, like a cottage in a book of fairy tales.

She entered, closed the door behind her, and locked it. Thad had said there would be a light switch on the wall to the right. She felt for it and turned it on, then looked around. The walls and carpeting were peach-colored. Before her was a staircase, to the left a dining room, and to the right, a living room. She walked in, rubbing the wall, feeling for the switch. When she found it, the room flooded with yellow light from recessed bulbs in the ceiling. The wall opposite the entranceway consisted of an enormous wall-to-wall, ceiling-to-floor unit with larger spaced shelves for big books toward the bottom and smaller spaced ones for paperbacks toward the top. There were potted plants scattered about but most looked brown and dry. Behind the simple coffee table and naugahyde couch was another wall of shelving with record albums and videocassettes. Opposite was the home entertainment center with stacks of fancy electronic components. "Wow!" she exclaimed, tempted to study all the dials, switches, meters, and smooth metallic surfaces.

Weslya opened the pouch on her belt and took out the folded papers that Thad had given her. The top sheet had the address and floor plan. The next one contained a list of instructions. The first thing she had to do was find the credit card. She walked to the record albums and ran her fingers across the spines. Good thing they were in alphabetical order. She followed the artists' names from Benny Carter to Cryin' Sam Collins, from John Coltrane to Reverend Gary Davis, until she came to Eric Dolphy. Who are all these people, she asked herself? She studied each album title by Dolphy until she got to the one called *Out To Lunch*. Pulling it from the shelf, she used her fingers like calipers, separating the twin sheets of cardboard. Holding it with the opening toward the floor, gravity released the plastic card, which fell to the carpet. She bent to retrieve it. The credit card went into her pouch and she restored the album cover to its place.

She glanced at the instruction sheet and followed the album spines until she came to the Mozart section. Placing the fingers of her left hand alongside symphonies six through ten, and her right hand fingers alongside numbers thirty-nine and forty, she pulled and the entire section came out as though they'd been glued together. She discovered that this was the case and also that there were no records within. A hollow had been carved from this block of cardboard and lodged inside were two videocassettes. She took them and replaced the block of empty covers.

Studying the list of instructions again, she left the living room after turning off the light, then walked up the staircase. At the top she turned right and walked into the bedroom. The curtains were open, the windows clean, the room bathed in warm sunlight. She fetched underwear, socks, and T-shirts from the bureau. Off of hangers in the closet she took jeans, button-down shirts, and a pair of tennis sneakers from the floor. From beneath the bed, she pulled a large plaid suitcase. After packing all of the clothing, she took the Walkman and a stack of audiocassettes from the night table, which she packed, along with the videocassettes, among the clothes for cushioning. Making certain that the lights were all off and that the front door would lock behind her, she left the house and started walking down the street.

The suitcase wasn't too heavy, but she was glad the car was just around the next corner. On the day that he'd been kidnapped, Thad had left it near the park where he went jogging every day. He was relieved to find it still there when they'd taxied over before driving Weslya to his house. Weslya walked right past Kurt and Sam, who ducked as she approached. Unaware that she'd been observed entering and departing, she turned the corner and kept walking until she reached the blue Ford with shining chrome. Weslya couldn't tell one car from another, but this one appealed to her sense of style. As she approached it, the trunk opened and she dropped the suitcase in and closed it. She got into the front seat.

"How did it go?" Kevin asked, sitting behind her.

"Smooth."

"Good," said Thad. "Did you see anybody suspicious hanging around?"

"Nope."

"Good." Thad gunned the engine and drove them to a motel on Market Street. It was a three-story U-shaped building with a parking lot in the center. Weslya and Kevin waited in the car while Thad got a room with his credit card. The three of them, Thad carrying the suitcase, trundled up the stairs and across the catwalk to room 331.

It was like the prototype of every motel room in America from coast to coast, Mexico to Canada; a thin carpet, twin beds with matching spreads, a television, desk, Gideon Bible, and paper-wrapped glasses in the bathroom. Thad offered Weslya her choice of the beds. She selected the one near the bathroom. Kevin sat in the chair by the desk and watched as Thad emptied the suitcase and Weslya sat on the bed, testing its bounce. Thad switched on the television set and turned the volume down to inaudible. The program in progress was one of the popular serial melodramas.

Weslya drew the curtains shut and returned to the bed. She pulled the velvet pouch from her leather pouch and rolled a thin joint.

"Hot damn!" said Kevin. "I haven't smoked the magical herb in almost three years. I guess it's about time to indulge again."

"We all deserve a break," said Thad.

As Weslya licked the flap, she explained, "This is my very special stuff. It's how I earn my living. I sell a few ounces a week and that gives me enough money to buy the food I don't grow and the clothing I don't make."

Thad grinned. "I guess you don't have to pay rent or utility bills."

"Not me. Living off the fat of the land."

She stuck the joint between her lips and lit the other end. After inhaling deeply, she handed it to Kevin. He drew deeply. "Um, this tastes good. Columbian?" He passed it to Thad.

"Nope. Weslyan."

Thad sucked in large lungfuls and passed it. "Weslyan?" he asked, exhaling.

"Yup. I don't even know where the seeds came from, but I use special fertilizer."

After Kevin's second hit, he looked at her, amazed, and said, "Girl, this stuff is powerful!"

She nodded.

"Agreed," said Thad as his eyelids grew heavy.

Weslya dinched the roach and stuck it in the velvet pouch.

"This is great," said Kevin.

"Wonderful," said Thad.

"So, what's the next step?" Weslya asked Thad.

"Wait a second," said Kevin, "what's the special fertilizer?"

"You won't believe it," she replied.

"Tell us," said Thad. "We're big boys. We can handle it,"

"You really want to know?" She looked from one face to the other. They nodded.

"Menstrual blood. Tampons, actually. I bury them with the seeds. You know, like the Indians would bury a dead fish with the corn. From pilgrim times? It works."

"Sure does," said Kevin, trying not to laugh.

"I'll say," said Thad. Then thought about it for a minute. He decided that it was probably the seeds — the "fertilizer" having nothing to do with it. But he didn't want to spoil the party, thought that Weslya was too nice to pick a fight with, so he didn't argue the point. Besides, there was a lot to do now that he had the necessities that Weslya had obtained. In a little while, after the initial rushes had passed, he'd discuss his strategy for exposing Corrigan.

☆ ☆ ☆

"Room 331," said Kurt, leaning against the pay phone.

"Stay with them," Corrigan barked. "If they split up, you guys separate and follow them. Just keep me posted."

"What if all three split up?"

"Stay with the guys. I don't give a shit about the girl. Probably some whore they're fucking."

"Yes, sir."

Kurt hung up the receiver and returned to the car, parked down the block from the motel on Market Street.

Sam asked, "What'd he say?"

"Stay with 'em."

"You hungry?"

Kurt hesitated. Admitting hunger might be considered a sign of weakness. But his body overruled his mind. "Yes."

"Good. Why don't you get us some food at that joint over there?" Sam pointed to a delicatessen across the street and down the block.

49

"What do you want?" Kurt resented Sam's bullying attitude, but he kept telling himself that a good soldier always bowed to superiors and patiently waited until a promotion catapulted him to a command position.

"Ham and cheese on rye with mustard. Two beers."

Kurt left to get the food. Sam turned over the Motley Crue tape, boosted the volume to ten, and pressed the start button.

☆ ☆ ☆

Nighttime had already descended when Kevin left the motel room. He'd spent the afternoon with Thad and Weslya, discussing possible battle plans. Finally, they'd decided they'd had enough for one day; they'd resume tomorrow. Kevin walked to the Castro district before returning to the guesthouse. There was a bar his friends had told him to visit. He'd have a drink, check out the scene, return to his room, and go to sleep. There was a great deal to be done the next day and he wanted to be rested and ready.

He entered the bar and ordered a Jack Daniels on the rocks. After a few sips, he turned to face the sparse crowd. It was early and there were only about fifteen guys scattered throughout the dimly lit room. A few played pool or video games. Most sat and talked.

The bar was almost exactly like many that he'd been to in New York. He'd expected, for no particular reason, that the bars here would be different from the ones back east. But he had the feeling that if you could pack this place up and ship it to New York, no one would know the difference. There were two kinds of bars: the bright, deco ones — fern bars — and the darker, sleazier kind — raunch bars. Every major city probably had at least one of each kind. This was one of the raunchier type. The guys wore denim or leather — not a designer label could be seen. The music was hard and loud. The only decoration was a photo of a muscular leatherman above the cash register.

"Hi."

Kevin turned his head and found a handsome blond with dazzling green eyes standing beside him.

"Hi."

They looked at one another, trying to figure out the best possible opening lines. *Do you come here often, what are you up to this evening, can I buy you a drink*, were very popular, if a bit worn out. Anything else seemed too pushy.

"Nice bar," said Kevin.

"It's okay."

The blond was drinking light beer from a can. Kevin was interested. This man was too attractive to pass up. And he seemed to be a nice guy.

"I'm from New York. Just visiting for a while."

"Never been there but I've always wanted to visit. The Big Apple, right? Boy, I've heard about some strange things going on there. Seems like an exciting place. I've lived here most of my life. It's a great town. I was born across the bay and I lived north of here for a while. But now I couldn't imagine living anywhere else."

"New York's okay. But if you can escape it now and then it's much more tolerable."

They talked for a while. About nothing special. Their eyes communicated the subtext of this discourse and eventually Kevin invited the man to spend the night at the guesthouse. He eagerly accepted. They left together and found a taxi. Neither the passengers nor the cabbie noticed that they were being followed.

Chapter 9

In her small room, early in the evening, Leona sat thinking. She felt lonely and unfulfilled. Yearning for the physical contact of a man, eager to visit with friends she hadn't seen for a while, anxious to punish Jack Corrigan and get on with her life, she thought of calling her friend, Paulette Bluefeather. Leona hadn't communicated with her in weeks. She'd feel better if she could speak with Paulette, who would soothe and reassure her. Paulette was resilient, compassionate, reliable. Leona could use some of her wisdom and strength. She'd call her and arrange a meeting so they could talk. Leona would tell her why she was working as a domestic and why she'd been so distant lately.

The telephone rang. Leona knew that Corrigan was home. The call was most likely for him. She'd let him answer it. When the telephone shrieked for the fourth time, Leona dashed out of her bedroom and into the kitchen. "Sí?"

"I gotta talk to Mr. Corrigan."

"I get."

She placed the receiver on the counter and hurried up the stairs. She knocked on the door to Corrigan's bedroom. "Señor Corrigan? Telephone."

"Okay," he shouted. Then, enunciating very slowly and clearly, "I'll . . . take . . . it . . . here . . . hang . . . up . . . downstairs."

Leona didn't want him to know that she understood, but figured it was the logical and typical thing to do. She went back downstairs and hung up the kitchen phone. Though tempted to listen in, she decided against it. If detected she might be fired. She returned to her bedroom and opened a book.

As soon as he heard the kitchen extension click off, Corrigan said, "Hello? Who is it?"

"Jack, it's Joe. Listen, I'm at the bar so I've gotta make

this quick. Actually, we should have this conversation in person but it can't wait."

"What's up, Joe? Nothing too serious I hope." Corrigan leaned back in the chair at his desk. He placed his pen alongside the ledger before him.

"Well," Joe hesitated, looked around to make sure no one could hear him. The crowd at the bar was large and noisy. He stuck a finger in his ear and faced the shelves of liquor bottles. Staring at the Pabst Blue Ribbon cardboard cut-out on the cash register, next to the hula doll, he spoke earnestly. "I gotta talk in code in case either of our phones are, well, you know."

"Yes, I know," he replied, exasperated.

"This is in reference to the last batch of, um, stuff."

"I'm listening." Corrigan grew impatient, angry, wishing he'd get to the point.

"Well, I've had some, ah, complaints. Some folks say it doesn't do anything. One guy said it made him sick."

"So, what's the big deal? They want their money back?"

"No, they're just threatening to go shopping elsewhere, if you know what I mean. I thought you should know."

"Jesus Fuckin' Christ. As if I didn't have enough problems. Look Joe, tell your people that you've spoken to your supplier and it'll be dealt with, okay? Tell 'em somebody probably made a mistake. All right? Meanwhile, I'll speak to my people and see what's happening. Okay?"

"All right. Sorry to bother you."

"Talk to you soon."

Corrigan went to the closet where the small safe was hidden. He got to his knees, his belly rubbing his thighs, dialed the combination and extracted a green tackle box. Opening it up, he grabbed the remaining packets of white powder and studied them. They looked normal. He didn't like the stuff himself and didn't want to try it. He trusted the people he got it from and had never had any complaints before. Maybe Joe was exaggerating? Or trying to pull a fast one? Corrigan considered the possibilities, then figured he'd get some other opinions. He'd give some to Kurt and Sam, see what they had to say about it. He'd sell some to Rosemary Bates and see if she squawked. After all, she was the expert. The stuff went through her like sand in an hourglass.

He'd wait for their reactions before contacting his dealer. They could get pretty rough and he didn't want to start any trouble. This new hassle, like all of the others, would eventually be dealt with and forgotten.

Corrigan teetered to his feet and returned to the desk. His attention was quickly captured by columns of figures and the calculator before him.

☆ ☆ ☆

When Kevin left the motel, Sam flipped a coin to see who would follow him. Kurt called heads and lost. Sam checked into the motel; an extra twenty dollar bill bought him a room opposite #331, on the same level, just across the parking lot. As Kurt drove off, Sam propped his feet up on the table and looked through the narrow slit in the curtains, wondering if the negro and the white chick were fucking. Probably, he said to himself. It was common knowledge that negro men were hot for white women, and the women were willing to oblige because the negro men had such large sex organs. It was obvious that they would be fucking, now that the queer was gone.

To alleviate the boredom of sitting by himself, Sam imagined all kinds of excruciating tortures for them. He saw himself pouring acid on them while they were in the act. That would be a sight to see. Or tying them up and setting them on fire. Bullets, unless strategically placed, would kill them too quickly. But carving them up with a sharp blade would be particularly painful, gruesome, and exciting. These fantasies ended when the light in #331 went out and no one exited. Sam figured they'd finished and were now asleep, so he dozed off and slept lightly, waking every time a sound penetrated his room. He'd open his eyes, gaze at the door and window under surveillance, then ease back into unconsciousness.

Kurt followed Kevin to a bar on Castro Street and waited until he emerged with a blond guy. They got into a taxi and Kurt followed them to the guesthouse. He spent the night at the steering wheel, trying to keep his mind busy. He made mental lists of all of the states of the union in alphabetical order, his favorite rock bands, all of the movies he'd seen since he was fifteen, and all of the cars — domestic and foreign — he hoped to someday own.

Kurt was twenty-three years old and still searching for his direction. As a child he'd dreamed of becoming a fireman. During his teenage years he'd planned to be a rock star. Now he didn't want to be anything. There was no occupation he knew of that appealed to him. So when he'd heard about the position that Jack Corrigan wanted filled, he'd applied. It sounded easy enough: driving his car, running errands, a room and two meals a day included. From what he'd heard about Corrigan he'd expected there would be some excitement involved. And sometimes there was. But mostly it was a pretty dull job: making pickups and deliveries, shopping for groceries, playing chauffeur, and a lot of waiting.

There had been the time that he'd helped Corrigan dump a body in the bay; the time he'd wound up in a brawl at Corrigan's bar. But mostly it was a lot of boredom: sitting around, playing delivery boy, and listening to Corrigan's endless speeches about money. What kept Kurt humming was the secret daydreams he indulged in when his mind was free to wander. Sometimes he was Green Lantern, charging his magic ring, or Superman, gazing through bank vaults with his X-ray vision. Occasionally he was Rambo, emerging victorious. But the best of all was when he was just himself, capable of doing anything he wanted to, whenever he wanted to do it.

☆ ☆ ☆

The morning sun poured through the window like dandelion wine. When Kevin opened his eyes, he felt better than he had in several days. He tried to recall the name of the man sleeping beside him. It started with a J. Was is Joshua? Jeremiah? No, Jeremy. That was it. They'd spent hours playing safe sex games and then, floating off to dreamland, they snuggled together like two tired puppies.

Kevin pulled his arm from beneath Jeremy's shoulders. Jeremy mumbled something and rolled onto his stomach.

Kevin slipped out of bed and went to the bathroom. When he returned, Jeremy was sitting on the edge of the bed, yawning and stretching. "Good morning."

They kissed, then Kevin asked him if he wanted to do breakfast. They showered together, dressed, and walked to the diner a few blocks away.

Over coffee, muffins, eggs, and bacon they told each other everything they'd been too shy to mention the night before. Kevin told Jeremy about his job with the art gallery in Soho, how much he was enjoying his vacation, but he was silent about the Corrigan caper and his new friends.

Kevin sipped some coffee and waited for Jeremy to balance the conversation.

"Since we're playing the truth game," said Jeremy, softly, his eyes pulling Kevin in like whirlpools, "I should tell you

55

right now that I hustle for a living, but let me add that last night I was off-duty."

Kevin nodded, indicating that he understood. "I guess some people get kind of upset when you tell them that."

"Do they ever. As soon as I get the words out they think I'm going to hand them an invoice. But, hey, sometimes it's for money and sometimes it's for me. I'm writing a book, based largely on my own experiences. Back in the sixties I was a typical West Coast hippie. And I thought I was straight. I was living in a crash pad with this terrific girl and then we moved to the country. But you're probably not interested in that."

"I am."

"I'll tell you about her some other time. Anyway I began to realize that what I was really interested in sexually was men. I occasionally have a female client when I'm tight for money, but it's not really what I'm into. Anyway, I realized I was gay and I really missed living in the city. So I moved back to town and worked in a restaurant and started writing. But there's more money in hustling than there is in waiting tables, so here I am. If I ever start making enough money writing, I'll quit the sex business. And I have enough juicy anecdotes to write a book about it. The other day, this Asian woman— very attractive—came into the gay bar that I usually work out of, not the place we were in last night, and paid me a lot of money to do some pretty weird stuff. I mean, we never even touched each other. She just wanted me to put her clothes on and then she called me names and watched me jack off. Very weird. But, hey, that's California."

Kevin found this man's story fascinating. His life seemed so routine by comparison. And he had no moral qualms about hustlers or prostitutes. They were as important to the fabric of society as policemen, school teachers, and retail clerks.

When they finished eating, they asked the waitress if they could borrow her pen and a couple of slips of paper. They exchanged addresses and telephone numbers. If they could get together again while Kevin was still in town, they would. If not, it had been wonderful. They paid the bill, left the diner, kissed, and separated.

It was such a bright and pleasant day, Kevin walked to the motel. He loved this city with its steep hills, trolley cars, excellent food, unusual architecture, and colorful history. Before coming, he'd read a great deal about it: The early settlers, the gold rush, the whale, seal, and oyster industries, the big earthquake, the beatnik poets and jazz musicians, the hippies and the summer of love. He'd always wanted to visit and now that he was seeing the city through his own eyes, he was enthralled at its energy, its texture, its colors, its traditions.

When he arrived at the motel, he knocked on the door to room #331. Weslya invited him in with a kiss on the cheek. "Gorgeous day," she said. "Ready for some new adventures?"

"Yes. I think. But nothing too dangerous . . . I hope we can nail that Corrigan asshole soon so I can get back to being a simple, carefree tourist."

She chuckled and sat on the rumpled sheets of her bed. Kevin sat on the rumpled sheets of Thad's bed.

A moment later Thad emerged from the bathroom with a towel around his waist. He turned on the television, exchanged good mornings with Kevin, and sat in the chair. The screen came alive with a soap opera already in progress. A very handsome actor took off his shirt, displaying the sculpted torso of a gym dandy.

"Wow!" Weslya exclaimed. "He's something else. They never used to have actors like that back when I watched this kind of stuff. And they never took their shirts off."

Thad harumphed. "These days actors don't have to read lines to audition for parts. They just take their clothes off. If they look like this guy, they get the job."

"Are you serious?" Weslya stared at him in disbelief.

"He's exaggerating," said Kevin. "But not by much. People don't want to see good acting anymore. Just beautiful faces and gorgeous bodies."

Weslya shook her head. "To think I've been missing stuff like this." She riveted her eyes to the screen. On his way into bed with an equally sexy actress, the actor stumbled over a line of dialogue. "Oh, well, I guess you can't have everything."

Thad rose from the chair and while collecting socks, underwear, a shirt, and jeans from the bureau drawers said, "Weslya needs to get some clothes."

"I didn't have time to pack," she giggled.

"What we should do is contact a detective with the police department I know and a reporter for the *Chronicle* who I know well and see if we can't get them to look at the video tape. If you two will back me up, offer to testify as eyewitnesses so they won't think I'm a kook making all of this up, maybe we'll actually make some progress."

"Sounds good," said Kevin.

"Ditto," Weslya agreed.

Thad went back into the bathroom to dress. Weslya changed the channel. Kevin leaned back against the headboard. They watched snippets of quizzes, soaps, and movies while waiting for Thad to get ready.

☆ ☆ ☆

After Kevin entered the motel room and the door closed, a bleary-eyed Kurt drove the car into the motel parking lot and went up to Sam's room.

"You look pretty well rested, pal," said Kurt. "I'm beat. Think I'll sack out for a while until we have to move again."

Sam looked through the phone book and picked up the telephone receiver. "I'm calling for some food. Want anything?"

"Yeah. Get me a coupla roast beef sandwiches, Russian dressing on rye, and two cokes."

"What happened last night?"

"He went to a bar and picked up some guy. Then they went to a house over on Larkin Street. They stayed there all night. Had breakfast this morning. That's all."

"Fuckin' queers." Sam shook his head. He dialed the delicatessen down the street while Kurt stretched out on the bed and closed his eyes.

Chapter 10

Organ music reached the decibel level of pain as Tom Slater stuck the knife into his chest, opening a vein just above his left nipple. As the glinting berries dribbled down his torso, Billy Bates, in his white altar boy costume, carried the collection tray from row to row, fixing his eyes on the face of each worshiper, just as his father had instructed. Dan Greenburg, who sat in the next to last row, had to dab tears from his cheeks with a handkerchief before he could reach into his pocket for a donation. When he'd first heard about the Church of Divine Forgiveness, he'd dismissed it with a raised eyebrow. But when his secretary had brought it up a second time and mentioned the commercial potential resulting from the recent media scandals involving televangelical sinners, he'd decided to see if perhaps she might be right. He laid a five-dollar bill on the tray and smiled at the boy. Billy did not return the smile, leaving Greenburg feeling disconcerted. All of the donors always wondered if they should have given more money. Some doubled their contribution the next time.

When the chapel had emptied, Greenburg walked up the aisle, stepped onto the stage, and entered the small room behind the curtain.

"Excuse me, Reverend Bates, my name is Dan Greenburg and I'm a producer with KWTV Channel 5."

The Reverend looked at the man in the custom-fitted gray suit with burgundy tie, an expensive corporate haircut, and patent leather shoes. "Pleased to meet you, Mr. Greenburg. How can I be of help?" The Reverend smiled and gave Tom a quick glance which said, beat it. He dutifully grabbed his shirt and left, whizzing by Greenburg without a word or nod.

"Is there someplace where we can talk?"

The Reverend spread his arms and looked heavenward. "What's wrong with the House of God?"

"N-nothing," Greenburg sputtered.

"Well then?"

Gathering his composure, Greenburg cleared his throat and began. "I was very moved by the performance, I mean the service, and it occurred to me that this might be perfect for broadcasting purposes. I was thinking along the lines of a weekly half-hour program—on a temporary basis until we can get some response and feedback. See if we can find some sponsors. See how the viewers react. If it flies, well, we might be interested in offering you a contract."

The Reverend saw thousand-dollar bills in his mind, spinning like the cherries in a slot machine. He wanted to clap his hands and shout for joy. But experience had taught him the value of a cool, reserved response to good news so, maintaining a neutral expression, he simply said, "It's a possibility. I must, of course, think it over and pray to God for guidance."

"I understand completely," said Greenburg with deference, almost bowing. "Certainly the details would have to be worked out very carefully. I just wanted to see if your initial reaction was favorable." He reached into his breast pocket and extracted a business card. "Call me after you've had time to consider my proposal and, of course," he pointed toward the ceiling, "after you talk it over with, you know, God."

"Yes, Mr. Greenburg. I'll call you as soon as I'm certain that it's the proper thing to do."

They shook hands and Greenburg backed out of the room. As soon as he was gone, Reverend Bates leaped into the air like a cheerleader and, raising his fist exclaimed, "Bull's-eye!"

He rushed upstairs and entered the living room. Billy was removing his gown, Rosemary counted the money on the collection tray. Turning off the television set, the Reverend faced his family and grinned. "Guess what?"

". . . fifty, sixty, seventy, seventy-five, eighty, eighty-one, eighty-two, what?" Rosemary placed the stack of bills on the table and scooped a handful of change.

"We're going to be on television!"

Billy stared at his father in utter disbelief.

Rosemary wasn't certain whether this was a joke. "Are they doing a documentary on downtown churches or something?"

"No. We're going to have our own television program. Every week. A half-hour long. At least temporarily. If it's a hit, we'll be doing it permanently."

"How much?" she asked, very interested.

"We haven't talked money yet. But I'm sure it will be something substantial."

"All of us are going to be on it?" Billy asked, scarcely believing. The Reverend smoothed the boy's hair. "Yes, son, all of us."

"Oh boy!"

"Well, this *is* good news," said Rosemary. "When do we start?"

"That hasn't been discussed yet either. In a couple of days I'll call the producer and get more details."

"Does this mean I can finally go to school?" Billy looked up at his father as if his whole life depended on the answer to this question.

"We'll see. It's possible." The Reverend did not want his son's mind poisoned by the communists who ran the public school system.

Billy hugged his father, then his mother, and ran into his bedroom. He jumped up and down on the bed with a gleeful smile.

Rosemary clasped her hands together after flinging the coins to the floor. "We've waited a long time for something like this."

"We've worked very hard and the producer is a smart businessman."

"Just like you, Larry."

"Just like me."

☆ ☆ ☆

When Thad was dressed, the television was turned off and he sat on the bed with the telephone directory splayed across his lap. First, he tried to contact Vince Pileggi, a reporter with the *Chronicle*. The receptionist informed him that Pileggi was not in his office. Would he like to leave a message? Yes. He gave the woman his name and the phone number of the motel.

Kevin and Weslya sat quietly, listening attentively to Thad's half of the conversation. There was nothing they could do except wait until the contacts had been made and some kind of appointments scheduled.

Thad hung up and thumbed through the directory in search of the proper precinct number. When he found it, he picked up the receiver and dialed. A male voice answered after two rings. "Sixth Precinct, Sergeant Jones speaking."

"Sir, may I please speak to Officer Andrew Bolkonsky?"

"Hold, please. I'll see if he's here."

Thad looked at his companions. "He's checking."

"Great," said Weslya.

"Finally getting somewhere," added Kevin.

"As soon as I get off the phone, we'll get you some new threads."

Weslya smiled.

"Officer Bolkonsky speaking, may I help you?"

"Andy? This is Thad Heath speaking. I don't know if you remember me, but we met about a year ago. I was working as a bartender at Sutter's Mill and you responded to a call to break up a fight?"

"I'm sorry, I don't recall . . . but what can I do for you?"

"Well, do you recall the disappearance of Enrique Ramirez? He was running for Board of Supervisors? It was a few months ago? In all the papers. Anyway, I have a video tape which proves that a certain Jack Corrigan, coincidentally, owner of Sutter's Mill, was responsible for his death. To make a long story short, this Corrigan character is now trying to kill me and two friends of mine so we won't spill the beans about the Ramirez murder. What we want to do is get together with you and show you the tape and tell you what we know — and get some protection."

"Do you wish to file a formal complaint?"

"Yes."

"Let me caution you, Mr. Heath . . ."

"Yes."

"Mr. Heath, that if this is a joke, I'll have you arrested for meddling in police affairs."

"This is no joke. Let us talk to you, show you what we've got. You'll see."

"Okay. How about three o'clock this afternoon?"

"That's fine with us. At the station house?"

"Yes. Just ask for me when you get here."

"Thank you. See you later."

Thad cradled the receiver. "It's all set. Three o'clock this afternoon."

☆ ☆ ☆

When he finished his ham and cheese sandwich, Sam crumpled the wax paper and tossed it into the greasy paper sack. He sat in the chair, listening to Kurt snore, watching the window across the way. This had become devastatingly boring and he was itching for some action.

He quietly left the room and slowly made his way around the catwalk above the parking lot. He passed rooms with tele-

62

visions blaring and rooms with the sounds of people moaning. When he arrived at the door marked #331, he knelt beneath the window after making sure no one was watching him.

He heard Thad talking to the policeman on the telephone and decided it was time to move. He hurried down to the car and opened the trunk, removed a gasoline can and water bottles, then went back to his room.

It took a few seconds to rouse Kurt.

"Hey, asshole, wake up."

While Kurt fought his way back to consciousness, Sam dialed Corrigan's number. He got a busy signal and slammed the receiver down.

"What's up?" Kurt asked, rolling to a sitting position.

"They've got the video tape and they're taking it to the cops. Corrigan's phone is busy. We've got to act fast."

Sam emptied two bottles of water into the bathroom sink and filled them with gasoline. Then he stripped a sheet from the bed, tore it into strips, and stuffed them into the bottlenecks.

"What are you doing?"

"Cocktails. See if you can get through to Corrigan."

Kurt dialed the number. "Still busy."

"Come on."

Kurt followed Sam out of the room. They moved quickly to a strategic spot not far from their target. Sam took a disposable lighter from his shirt pocket and lit the tails hanging from the bottles. He handed a flaming glass torch to Kurt. "On the count of three. Okay?"

Kurt nodded.

"One. Two. Three."

They hurled the bottles at the window of room #331. The glass shattered and screams could be heard from within. Sam and Kurt ran back to their own room and closed the door. As they looked out across the parking lot, they could see smoke pouring out of the broken window, drifting in billows up toward the sun. Orange and yellow shards of flame devoured the billowing curtains, dragon's tongues of fire lapped at the outside wall above the window frame.

Kurt looked at Sam. "Good show, partner."

"That oughta take care of those fuckers," he smirked.

63

Chapter 11

When enough pressure builds up within a vessel, an escape must be found or it will explode. And Leona was feeling more and more like she was filling up with anxiety and loathing, pressing outwardly from her heart. She'd been too patient for too long. Questions demanded answers, justice had to be balanced, and a period of mending and repair would eventually be necessary. So Leona finally decided to wrest whatever incriminating information she could find, leave Corrigan's forever, and try to get the attention of the proper authorities.

She pulled on her bathrobe and tied the belt, then walked stealthily past the living room. Suzie slept on the couch, the blinds drawn, the room dark, the house quiet. Leona didn't know where Corrigan was, but he was surely not at home. She crept up the stairs and entered the bedroom. As soon as she was seated at the desk, she took out some files that she hadn't looked at the first time.

There were green tinged sheets of paper with columns and entries in the thousands of dollars. One stack labeled Outgoing, the other, Incoming. In the first one were duplicates of checks, mostly for bills and payroll. None for any of the organizations Corrigan was reputedly funding. The Incoming file had large cash deposits, all marked with a "C." Leona compared the final figures of the two sets of calculations. It was clear Corrigan was making huge amounts of money and spending very little.

Leona was about to reach for more files when she heard a sound coming from behind her. Turning her head, a flat palm hit her cheek, sending her flying out of the chair. She hit the floor and rolled a few feet. Suzie stood over her, fists clenched, her eyes throwing off sparks. Her long, black hair, usually so perfect, looked frazzled and wild. Leona looked up at her, cowering, her heart beating in double time. Her jaw ached and there was a sharp pain at her hip where she'd struck the floor. Still reeling, her mind attempted to grasp the situation.

"Just wait'll I tell Jack about this!" Suzie barked. "He'll have you skinned alive!"

Leona glanced down at her feet, just a few inches from Suzie's ankles. Solid images came into focus in her mind. Instinctively, Leona shot out her foot and hooked it around Suzie's closest ankle. She jerked back and Suzie toppled to the floor. Leona was instantly on top of her, pinning her shoulders to the carpet with her knees. She slapped her face, then grabbed Suzie's hair and yanked her to her feet. Before Suzie could realize what was happening, Leona flung her into the closet where she crumpled like a wet rag doll. Leona slammed the door and hooked the back of the chair underneath the doorknob. The sound of fists on wood and a screechy voice came from behind the closed door.

With that done, Leona tucked the files under her arm. She hurried downstairs, got dressed, and packed her suitcase. Then she left the house and took the bus to the home of her friend, Paulette Bluefeather.

Sitting in the shaky, slow-moving bus, Leona wondered if she'd done the right thing. Now Corrigan would be after her. Would he kill her like he'd killed Enrique? She'd have to get help from the police or leave town. Otherwise she'd walk forever on uncertain ground, every moment fearing that just ahead was a straw-covered pit with sharp stakes pointing skyward, waiting for her flesh and blood. Images of herself, corpse-like, punctured, bloodied, rose in her mind. Her spine chilled and goosebumps appeared on her arms.

She arrived at the small white house on top of a steep hill. Paulette, a heavyset woman with big eyes and a colorful neckerchief tied around her hair, opened the door. She hugged Leona and welcomed her. They entered and Paulette locked the door.

Leona put the suitcase down and looked at her friend with desperation. "Can I stay a few days?"

Paulette clasped her hands together. "Of course. For as long as you like. What's wrong?"

Leona sighed. "I just need to think about things."

"Stay as long as you like," said Paulette, knowing she'd eventually hear the entire story. She fixed a pot of herbal tea while Leona unpacked her suitcase.

☆ ☆ ☆

When the bottles with flaming streamers crashed through the motel room window, the gasoline splattered, throwing missiles of liquid fire in all directions. Weslya's dress started burning like tinder. She swatted at the flames like buzzing insects that she could chase away. But the taunting fire clung to her, singeing her arms. Panicking, she shrieked and her hands flew to her head, bundling her hair to keep it from igniting. Thad immediately snapped into action and wrapped his arms around her, then dove to the floor, rolling on top of her. Kevin grabbed a blanket and threw it over her, Thad helping to smother the burning fabric.

Meanwhile, the room filled with smoke. It stung their eyes and singed their lungs. Red-eyed, coughing, and choking, the three of them made for the door and lunged out onto the catwalk, gasping for breath. Kevin grabbed Weslya by the shoulders. "Are you all right?"

She looked down at her charred dress, then examined her arms. "Fuck, I think so."

Thad leaned over the railing, coughing, fighting for air. Kevin placed his arm around his shoulder. "You okay?"

Thad nodded. "I'll be fine, soon's I catch my breath." He winced, wondering if he'd ever be able to stop fighting. He'd been gassed and beaten in civil rights demonstrations, wounded in Vietnam, mugged on a dark city street, kidnapped at gunpoint in broad daylight, and now this. Would there be a time to just live in peace?

Sirens screamed in the distance and a few moments later two firetrucks pulled up. Firemen snaked hoses up the stairs and the room was doused with hard streams of water. As the flames were subdued, two women from the fire department asked the victims questions and recorded the answers on clipboards. One was Japanese-American, a short, plump woman with a new wave haircut. On her chest was a plastic name badge reading Erika Hong. The other, Drexel Johnson, was black, taller and lean, with an Afro do.

Drexel Johnson paced, arms akimbo, firing questions at them as though they were defendants on trial. "Who started the fire?"

"Hell, we don't know," gasped Thad.

"Not us," said Kevin, his arm wrapped around Weslya's shoulder. She was too frightened to say anything.

66

"Do you know who *might have* done it?"

"Not a clue," said Kevin.

Thad almost said something but held back.

"Have any of you been involved in any other fires during the past twelve months?"

"No," said Thad.

Weslya and Kevin shook their heads.

"Take these cards." The two firewomen each produced three cards and handed one to each of the victims. "If you remember anything or notice anything funny, call us," said Erika, her voice smooth, her eyes compassionate.

"We're going to investigate thoroughly," said Drexel. "And when we find out who's responsible," she stuck the clipboard between her knees, clenched the pencil between her teeth and slammed her fist into her palm, "BAM! We're going to get 'em."

She looked comical, speaking around the pencil. Thad laughed.

"What's so funny?" she spat.

Thad pointed at her. "You. With that pencil in your teeth." She removed the pencil and twisted her face up as though she'd sucked on a lemon.

Then she looked at her partner.

"Well, I have to admit," Erika suppressed a giggle, "it probably did look kind of funny." Drexel scowled, turned away, and walked down the stairs. Erika shrugged her shoulders, turned, and followed.

The motel manager approached the victims. "The firemen have informed us that this was not your fault. We will gladly provide a different room at the same rate."

Thad and Weslya returned to the room, soggy and sooty now, collected their belongings, wet but otherwise undamaged, and were then led to room #323.

Closing the door behind them, Kevin sat in the chair, Weslya sprawled on a bed and Thad spread his wet clothing out on any available surface, including the television set. "This stuff should dry pretty soon. It's only damp."

"Well, I need to relax a little after that unexpected surprise," said Weslya. "And then I definitely need to get some new clothes."

They sat in silence, thinking about what had happened and what they should do. Thad felt that they should split up, as they were obviously being followed. Kevin wanted to get the videocassette into the hands of the police as soon as possible so he could resume his vacation. Weslya was eager to see this man face to face, this Corrigan, the one who'd caused so much trouble and never showed himself.

"We should split up," said Thad. "We're being followed."

Weslya said, "That's a good idea, but first I have to get something new to wear."

Kevin looked back and forth at the two of them. "What we should do is get the video to the cops right away and leave the rest to them. And while it's on my mind, what's on the tape anyway?"

Thad sat on the other bed. "There's two parts. One is of Corrigan, not realizing there was a camera present, blackmailing two illegal aliens. The other part is sort of Enrique Ramirez's last will and testament with his statement that he suspects Corrigan is trying to kill him."

"And what happened to Enrique Ramirez?" Weslya asked.

"He disappeared. We suspect his body was thrown into the bay."

"Look," said Kevin, "each of us can do what we want. I'll take the video to the cops. Thad, you can create a diversion by just driving around in circles. Wes, you can shop for clothes. If anyone's following us, they'll have quite a job. We can meet later for dinner and bring each other up-to-date."

Weslya nodded with enthusiasm. "Sounds good to me."

Thad agreed. "Good thinking."

They left a few minutes later and separated.

☆ ☆ ☆

Kurt and Sam watched as Thad, Kevin, and Weslya emerged from the room and walked down the stairs to the parking lot.

"There they go," announced Kurt, like a kid at the racetrack.

"Tell me something I don't know," said Sam.

Kurt scrunched his nose at him when Sam wasn't looking.

They left their room and peered out over the guardrail outside the door. As Thad started the car, Weslya turned right, walking away from the motel, while Kevin turned left.

Kurt and Sam looked at one another.

"What do we do now?" Kurt displayed a touch of panic in his voice. With a look of self-satisfaction, Sam said, "Just like Corrigan told us, we follow the guys."

"I'll flip you for the car," said Kurt.

He flipped a quarter. Sam called, "Heads!"

68

"You win," said Kurt, crestfallen.

Sam sprinted to the car, started it, and followed Thad down Market Street. Kurt, on foot, stalked Kevin, keeping about half a block behind him. It was mid-afternoon and the sun was at its highest point, flushing the shadowy city with light, as the earth continued turning away from the sun.

Chapter 12

It was dark and stuffy in the closet. Once Suzie had resigned herself to captivity, she felt around to see if she could find anything which might help her escape. But first, she cleared the shoes from beneath her and stacked them against the wall. Feeling a bit more comfortable, she pushed all of the hanging clothes to one side so she could stand up.

She'd traveled a great distance from where she'd started out, to arrive at where she now stood. Her childhood had been very quiet and solitary. At school she felt estranged from the other kids; they'd never heard of Thailand or Paris. And most of them were white, affluent, with that overbearing confidence found in many well-to-do Americans. Suzie withdrew, refused to compete or commiserate, and relied upon her own imagination for companionship.

But once she'd grown and left for college, her life began to blossom. She found that she could easily attract men and mold them to her designs. That is, until they rebelled and fought her, resulting in a harsh and recriminatory break-up. Tensions between Suzie and Jack Corrigan had reached the point where one of them must bend and accommodate or the relationship would splinter into a mass of sharp edges.

Suzie began kicking at the door, pounding on the four walls, stamping her feet, shouting for help. It was impossible for her to tell how long she'd been confined but it seemed like an eternity had transpired before she heard a muffled voice, the sound of wood scraping wood, the turning of the doorknob. Corrigan stood there, perplexed. She angrily told him about Leona's treachery, then went to the bathroom, changed her clothing, and met him in the living room.

He was already drunk by the time she got there. His eyes had that watery look and his face was pink, white, and splotchy like strawberry yogurt. He offered her a drink. She accepted.

And tried not to look at his face as he seated himself and started talking.

"Well, it looks like the Cuntessa of Guacamole has packed her burro and hat-danced herself away from our humble hacienda. The bitch. First we've got to find her. Get my files back before she shows 'em to anybody. Then kill 'er."

Suzie looked at the folds of his neck and said, "And who's supposed to take care of that? You've got Sam and Kurt chasing the others and you're too drunk to spit. If you think *I'm* going to try and find her, guess again." She threw back her head and downed the remainder of her drink.

"You'll do whatever I tell you to do, when I tell you to do it, or I'll send a letter to your father which will surely destroy any chance you might have of collecting your inheritance."

Suzie slammed the glass down on the table. "Asshole!" she spat and moved out of the room with the determination and single-mindedness of a wind-up toy.

"Don't you dare take the car!" Corrigan shouted.

Suzie slammed the front door shut, scooped the car keys from her purse, and got in the car. She drove to the Water Works, hoping to find the blond guy that she'd rented before. But he wasn't there. Nor could she find any other hustlers who were willing to leave with her. Money was not the obstacle. She had plenty. But none of the guys were interested.

She left the bar in a huff and drove to another place that she'd heard of once. It was called Handcuffs and, according to the rumors, people looking for rough, kinky action could find it there.

The place had no sign outside, but a drunk stumbling around in the vicinity gave Suzie directions after she paid him a dollar. She found the place and walked down the stairs to a dark, damp dungeon of a cellar. There were stocks, a guillotine, whips, and chains suspended from the ceiling. Sitting at the bar was a girl with tracks all over her arms. The barmaid and waitress wore black leather corsets, seamed hose, and had safety pins in their ears. At a small table in the corner sat a young-looking man with a scar on his cheek. Suzie walked over to him. "Can I buy you a drink?"

"Yeah," he smiled goofily.

"What do you want?"

"Black Russian."

She went to the bar, ordered two, paid for them and sat down at the table.

"Thank you," he said, taking a sip.

Suzie tasted it and gagged. Too sweet. Like liquid sugar with a burning aftertaste. "You drink this stuff often?"

"Now and then," he replied.

"What's your name?"

"Tom. Yours?"

"Suzie."

They looked at one another. She knew it was her move. "I've got the money if you've got the time and place."

"I've got the time. As far as the place goes—we'll have to sneak in."

"Sneak in where?" This aspect of it interested her. There was something about doing things you weren't supposed to do that she found exciting.

"The Church of Divine Forgiveness. Over on Van Ness."

Suzie lit a cigarette. "I thought I recognized you. You're the featured attraction in Reverend Bates' Spectacle of Horrors."

"That's one way of looking at it," he said defensively. "Pays good though," he added, to justify his participation.

"How tough is it to sneak in?"

"I do it all the time."

They left the bar and Suzie drove them to the church. She parked a few blocks away. There was a Mass in progress. The Reverend and his son were on stage. The wife was operating lights and music in the rear. Tom and Suzie snuck up the stairs. "How come you're not working today?" Suzie whispered.

"Cause my blood supply is limited and the Reverend knows its best not to overdo it."

They entered his small room on the third floor. It was bare except for a naked light bulb in the center of the ceiling, a cardboard box of clothing, and a thin mattress on the floor with a yellowed pillow.

Suzie took off her blouse, her beaded bracelet, her spiked heels, and her fishnet stockings. She unhooked her bra, wriggled out of it, and dropped her panties. She stood before him with perfect skin, firm breasts like alabaster peaches, her waist slender, hips shapely, ankles delicate.

"Strip!" she commanded.

He removed his T-shirt, moccasins, jeans, socks, and bikini briefs. His body was lean and wiry. Tufts of black hair sprouted from his underarms, his chest, and his crotch. He had

72

scars along the length of his arms and several on the inside of his thighs.

"You like to bleed?"

"It gets me off every time."

"It's not faked?"

"Watch." He fetched a penknife from his pants pocket, opened it and bent to cut an incision in his left calf. He straightened up and dropped the knife to the floor. As the crimson beads ran from his leg down his ankle to the floor, his penis began to stir, lengthen, and stand out from his body. A few seconds later he trembled from neck to feet and spurted a dollop of semen to the floor.

Tom looked at Suzie with a satisfied grin, as if to say, I told you so.

"Will it work if *I* do it?" she asked, feeling a tightening in her stomach. When she'd seen him cut himself during the church service she'd felt nauseous. Seeing it now, she was fascinated. "Do you have an orgasm every time?"

He nodded enthusiastically.

"Does the Reverend know?"

Tom shook his head. "No. He never asked. No one does and I guess you can't tell just by looking at me. If I have my clothes on."

Suzie stooped and picked up the knife. She moved closer to him. Gazing at his eyes with a hypnotic stare, she asked, "If I cut you will you fuck me?"

He nodded.

She placed the point of the blade against the warm skin above his left nipple. He flinched and closed his eyes. She pressed it into the skin. It gave, like a dimple, then broke. Blood dripped down his chest.

Suzie dropped the knife and lay on the mattress. He knelt down, mounted her, and pumped his hips. Suzie looked at the blood smearing her breasts. She gasped. The room started spinning and she felt lighter than cotton. She closed her eyes and grabbed the mattress sides with her hands as her body convulsed in rapid spasms. She saw a laser show in her mind and felt like a river of hot honey running down the side of a steep hillside, settling in a cool, calm pool. She sighed with satisfaction.

Tom felt elated that he'd been able to shoot twice in such a short span of time. Part of him wanted to do it again, just to see if he could. The other part was wary that he'd reveal himself to be greedy and foolish. He remained silent, hoping she would decide what was to happen next.

She dressed and paid him. "Are you going to help me sneak out of here?"

"Yes, ma'am. Whatever you say." He picked up his clothes and put them on.

"Do you suppose we can do this again some time?" she asked, coy and deferential.

"If you like," he replied, suppressing his eagerness.

They left the building as the collection tray passed among the congregation.

☆ ☆ ☆

Corrigan sat in the kitchen drinking his fourth cup of coffee. He was feeling a little better now. After Suzie had gone, he kept drinking straight vodka until he passed out. When he awoke several hours later, he'd stumbled into the kitchen and groggily fixed a pot of coffee. After drinking three cups, he made himself two thick bologna and lettuce sandwiches dripping with mayonnaise and mustard. Halfway through the last cup of coffee, the telephone rang. Corrigan got up from the chair and pulled the receiver from the white wall phone. The cord stretched twenty-five feet so he had no trouble sitting again. "Yes?"

"Jack — it's Larry Bates. How are you?"

"Not too bad, Reverend. Got my share of problems like anyone. But nothing to keep a good man down. What's up?"

"Well, Jack, hold onto your hat, I've got great news. There's a television producer, goes by the name of Dan Greenburg, wants to give the church a weekly half-hour broadcast."

There was a momentary silence as the Reverend's words penetrated the innermost recesses of Corrigan's cloudy brain.

"You mean, every week, for a half-hour, you'll do a show on television?"

"That's right."

"Lots of money, I suppose?"

"Lots."

Corrigan's face broadened into a smile. "Just when I needed some good news."

"This *is* good news. Not only will we get money from the show, but more people will come to see us in person. It's like getting paid and getting free publicity at the same time. God *does* work in mysterious, miraculous ways!"

"I suddenly have a million questions, Reverend. Like when does all of this start? How much do we get per show? And of course, you and I will have to put our heads together and see what kind of breakdown we should have between us."

"Of course, Jack. You know me. I wouldn't try to cheat you."

"I know that," Corrigan said, not really believing, but in no mood for an argument. He was certain the Reverend was skimming the daily donations.

"I'm meeting this guy Greenburg in a few days. I'm sure there'll be contracts to sign and such. As soon as I have more information I'll let you know all the details."

"Thanks for the good news."

"My pleasure. And God bless."

Corrigan rose to replace the telephone receiver. He sat down again and finished the cold coffee in his cup.

Life is a constant struggle for control. Nature, government, society will put you in a straitjacket and batter you with billy clubs unless you take things into your own hands and exert your will. Jack Corrigan's parents had tried to keep him in his place, the army had almost broken his spirit, his first employer had been a tyrant. So he'd quit working at the bowling alley and had gone into business for himself. He stole collection cans for leukemia, cerebral palsy, cystic fibrosis, and other charities. And never once thought that this might be wrong; he was simply taking control of his life. When he saw how easy it was to make scads of money without having to answer to anyone, account for anything, punch a time clock, his mind began to develop new schemes which would insure his peace and freedom.

But it was time to start thinking about the future. Money was coming in from the coke but that had to be investigated. The last thing he needed was to get a reputation for bad stuff. Maybe the suppliers were trying to pull a fast one? Or maybe it was just a mistake. He'd have to find out. The church business was doing great. In a few weeks there'd be a new church upstate. More money. The bar business was only doing moderately well. It seemed to go up and down following no particular pattern. Too large an investment would be required to turn the joint into a real money-maker. But now the wetback bitch had the files and Heath was on the loose with the videotape. It's time to take decisive action, he instructed himself. I've got to see if I can get the files and the tape — and then I've got to get away somewhere. Things are getting too complicated. Let the businesses take care of themselves for a while and just collect the profits. Maybe San Diego? Seattle? But who can I trust? Suzie is too high-strung and rebellious. Sam, Kurt, and Joe are too stupid. If I go away, the Reverend will rob me blind. The coke will get snorted instead of sold. The bar will go out of business in two months. I need someone I can trust. Or better yet, someone I can control. Someone who did something wrong that I can prove. And if they try to screw me, I'll turn 'em in. That's what I need. A desperate, vulnerable, not too smart, scared, gullible criminal.

Chapter 13

It felt so good to be back in town. Weslya had lived on Haight Street for over three years after moving west from Indiana. She'd painted colorful birds on her face, tried every street drug that came within her orbit, had sex with men, women, and men and women. Then she'd met the man who'd convinced her that they'd be happier living in the country. They'd left the city and, after a couple of years, he'd left her. So, she'd decided to stick it out by herself. She was tired of the craziness of the city; the bad drugs, the violent kids, the mean policemen. But after more than ten years of solitude, reflection, purification of her mind and spirit, she was glad to be back in the teeming metropolis.

She had plenty of cash in her leather pouch and it was time to buy some new clothes. Whenever she'd left her cabin to buy supplies at the shopping center in the valley, she'd see women in crazily colored, comfortable-looking pants, or tight, formfitting jeans. Some of them wore suede ankle boots and had strange hairstyles that looked off-center, but very fashionable. She was ready to join this army of new women who appeared to be rebelling against the slick, elitist look that they'd been raised to worship.

First she entered a boutique and bought jeans, a pair of colorful cotton slacks, two loose-fitting blouses, and a sensible skirt. She threw her burnt dress in the trash and left the store wearing the jeans and muslin peasant blouse embroidered with flowers and vines. With her belt and pouch around her waist, she looked strong and independent.

Next, she stopped in a shoe store and bought a pair of black suede ankle boots. She couldn't believe how comfortable they were. The saleslady wrapped Weslya's worn sandals in the shoebox and she left wearing the new boots. Catching her reflection in a shop window, she liked the look of her new ensemble. Casual and sexy, new and fashionable, she was up-to-date and felt more confident and assured than she had in quite a while.

She wandered around near Union Square enjoying the sights, sounds, weather, the pedestrians, the vehicles, the vendors, the buildings. Everything. So much had changed. The streets were cleaner now. The people thronging the crowded sidewalks were more diverse than they had been before. New buildings, many with mirrored glass and chrome, had been erected, giving the city an almost futurist look. Weslya was enthralled by everything. She felt like a child at the circus.

After spotting a hair salon, she walked in and approached the receptionist. "Hello. I'd like to have my hair styled, please."

The skinny woman with green hair looked at Weslya's long, unfettered locks and said, "My first opening is Thursday at 4:00."

"That's in three days. Are you joking?"

"No," replied the receptionist, a bit huffily.

"Thanks, anyway," said Weslya. Fuck it, she thought, the hair could be cut any time.

She left the salon and continued wandering around. She had almost four hours to fill before meeting Thad and Kevin. She wondered how they were doing. Fine, she supposed. They both seemed so capable.

When she happened to glance at a theater marquee, it occurred to her that she hadn't been to see a movie in years. The sign said *Killers From Beyond* and *Pretty Dead*. They sounded like fun films. She bought a ticket and walked into the darkness. When she found a place to sit, she stuffed her bundles beneath the seat, then went to buy popcorn, a chocolate bar, and soda pop. Leaning back comfortably, wide-eyed and feeling good all over, she let herself go and merged with the moving images on the large screen.

☆ ☆ ☆

It didn't take Thad very long to realize that he was being followed. He had, of course, suspected that he would be. But he didn't think his pursuer would make it so obvious. After he'd made three right turns in rapid succession, it was evident that the red Toyota intended to stick to him like Velcro. He decided he might as well have some fun.

He gunned the engine and crossed Market Street heading northwest. When he got to the top of the hill on Jackson Street, he pulled to the curb and waited for the trolley. Glancing into his rearview mirror, he noted that the chase vehicle had double-parked about ten car lengths behind. Thad grinned, then placed a cassette into the dash unit. A jaunty saxophone melody began to pour forth from the quadrophonic speaker system as a cable car turned the corner and headed down Jackson toward Fisherman's Wharf.

Thad shifted gears and tore off. When the cable car reached the next intersection, he swerved around it, leading it down the hill. At the next intersection, he made a sharp right, executed a frenzied three-point turn, narrowly avoided colliding with a bus, then waited for the red car to pass by. He turned onto the street right behind the import and rode along on its tail. The driver, Sam, hadn't noticed that he was now being followed. So Thad honked his horn in five quick jabs. When Sam glanced at his rearview, Thad waved to him and smiled. Sam scowled and skidded to a halt. Thad kicked his brake quickly enough to prevent any severe damage, but not enough to prevent contact. The fenders bumped. Thad threw his car into reverse and backed into a side street. Then he drove off slowly enough so that he could easily be followed.

This pattern was repeated throughout the afternoon. Thad would wait until Sam had caught up with him. Then he'd find a way to come up behind him. Their bumpers would connect, then Thad would make a quick departure.

As the sun began to sink behind the hills, and the valleys were draped with shadows, it occurred to Thad he should prevent his pursuer from discovering the location of his rendezvous with Kevin and Weslya. So he fired up his engine and tore off toward Embarcadero. It was easy to lose the Toyota in among all of the trucks, buses, and other vehicles. When he was certain he was no longer being tailed, Thad drove to the guesthouse, but parked several blocks away so that his car wouldn't lead any unwanted persons to this location.

☆ ☆ ☆

Clutching a manila envelope with the important videocassette inside, Kevin walked toward the police station of the Sixth Precinct. Adrenaline flooded his system, his senses on alert for signs of surveillance or pursuit. Nothing seemed threatening or unusual. He checked his wristwatch. He had plenty of time to get there for his meeting with the sergeant. And he still wanted to absorb all of the sights of this dangerous and beautiful city before it was time to return home. So, like the tourist he was supposed to be, he lingered and stopped whenever anything grabbed his attention.

The main thing that attracted him was the architecture. After checking out several clothing and book stores, it became clear that the same products — whether pants, shirts, or novels, magazines — were available to the public on the West Coast and on the Eastern Seaboard. Just as the bars had failed to display any differences from the ones he was familiar with in New York, it appeared that everything else was similar as well. He'd expected that there would be vast regional differences. And perhaps, in the boondocks there were. But the major cities of America, he gathered, were all stocked by the same handful of corporations which were imposing a bland uniformity on the various populations.

But buildings, if constructed properly, can last a long time. And many were built long before the currently powerful corporations were born. So Kevin took pleasure from the homes and public buildings that he passed on the way. The civic architecture was grand and cosmopolitan. But domiciles were charming and ethnic. He saw houses that looked English, Italian, or Mexican. There were hybrids of these as well and some that looked like they'd been carted intact from small New England or Midwestern towns. Kevin wished he'd brought a camera, then recalled that he'd never snapped a decent photo in his life.

When he arrived at the police station, he passed through the metal detector and asked for Sergeant Bolkonsky. He was told that the sergeant was out on a personal emergency. Kevin asked if he could leave the package for him. The answer was affirmative. He wrote a brief note of explanation, placed it in the envelope with the cassette, and left it with the officer behind the desk.

As he walked to the guesthouse, his mood evolved from disappointment to anger. He'd hoped that the tape would be seen immediately and the culprits dealt with right away. But now it looked as though his vacation was to be postponed indefinitely. He reminded himself that he wasn't having such a bad time. He liked Thad and Weslya — both so refreshing compared to his friends back home. Too many of his relationships had become stale. Here were two nice people — with backgrounds very different from his own — whose company he enjoyed immensely. Thad was so smart, in control and a wonderful adversary for verbal jousts. Weslya so sweet, innocent, and accepting of anything odd that crossed her path.

Still, there was the constant threat of danger. Bullets and firebombs hadn't been included in his travel plans. And real safety would only come when Corrigan and his gang were behind bars.

Chapter 14

About once every two or three weeks Reverend Bates left his church immediately after the six o'clock Mass to attend an Alcoholics Anonymous meeting at a nearby public high school. It was at these times that Rosemary planned to have Jack Corrigan stop by with a few grams of coke. Her husband would announce to her, usually the day before, that he was leaving directly after the next evening's service. Rosemary would sneak into the bedroom while he was watching television, call Corrigan, and tell him that she needed a shipment the following evening.

At around seven-thirty Corrigan arrived. His white hair was wind-buffeted and in need of a trim. As he lurched his bulk up the stairs to the second floor of the church building, Rosemary stood at the top of the landing in a billowy house dress with tiny parasols all over it, her face stripped of makeup, her hair flattened back with oily conditioner.

Although she didn't look perky and fluffed-up, as usual, Corrigan felt a pang of desire. He was certain she was attracted to him and always flirted shamelessly. Rosemary assumed that he was interested in her and responded similarly. But they'd never gotten beyond the stage of verbal and gestural foreplay because he presumed she was devoted to her husband and she believed that he was obsessed with Suzie. This made their flirtations seem safe and innocent.

"Where's the li'l' mudpie?" asked Corrigan as he shifted himself, panting, off the last step.

"He's already asleep. Sometimes he gets so tuckered out after the last show."

"You look lovely tonight."

Rosemary blushed. Her lips curled back to reveal sparkling white teeth. She laughed. "Go fish!" she said with true modesty as her hands flew to arrange her hair, which she suddenly remembered, was not fit for company. "Shall we go into the living room?" She turned quickly and led him down the hall. They sat on the couch and Corrigan reached into his jacket pocket for six grams. Rosemary extracted a wad of bills from her slipper and gave it to him, then placed the tiny packets in her side pocket.

"This is some special new stuff and I want your opinion," he said.

"What's special about it?"

"A little less filler than usual. I'm trying a new supplier," he lied.

"Oh." She took a cigarette from the pack on the table and lit it with a gold-plated lighter. "Well, I'm sure I'll like it. I always do."

"Good. Why don't you try some now?"

"Okay." She rose and went to the bathroom, locking the door behind her. Corrigan had intended for her to do it right there. He'd always wanted to watch her. He didn't know why, he just thought it might be interesting to see. But it was unthinkable for her to do it anywhere except by herself behind a locked door. After all, she had her reputation to protect.

Corrigan glanced at the pretty women in the advertisements of the magazine on the table. When Rosemary returned he guiltily closed it.

"Well, what do you think?" she asked.

"I don't know yet." She sat. "Takes a few minutes to feel it." There was an awkward silence of several second's duration. Finally she said, "So, tell me, how's everything?"

He sighed and leaned back. "Lots of problems lately. But nothing you want to hear about." He thought of Suzie and all of their recent quarrels. Then he wondered where Kurt and Sam were. He hadn't heard from them in hours. And where was Leona whatshername with his files? Too much to deal with.

Rosemary patted his jelly-like, khakied thigh with concern. "Poor Jack. We all have our problems. They usually work themselves out."

When he felt the warmth of her hand it triggered something in his mind. He leaned forward and draped his arm around her neck. She had to struggle against the weight.

"You know, Rosemary, sometimes I think that you're the only person in the entire world who truly understands me." He looked at her with all of the solemnity he could muster.

She looked away, as though this were too great a burden to bear.

82

"I mean it," he said and pulled her body alongside his. The angle of her spine in this position was too uncomfortable. She shifted her buttocks closer to him to alleviate the strain. Corrigan interpreted this move as an invitation. He pulled her face toward his and kissed her on the lips. His tongue darted out like a frog's and licked her teeth. She jerked back in surprise, as though touched by a cattle prod. Corrigan figured she was turned on and his to take.

"What are you doing?" She pulled away.

He pulled her back. "Allowing a precious moment to happen," he whispered seductively.

"I don't know," she said. Then it occurred to her that if she didn't respond in a friendly manner, he might kick her family out of their church or cut off her supply of brain tabasco. I'll play along for the sake of the family's stability, she told herself. And placed her finger on her lips to indicate silence, then led him to the bedroom and quietly closed the door.

He'd never seen this room before, with its blinding whites and deep reds. It reminded him of a valentine card. They lay on the quilted bedspread. Suddenly Corrigan wondered if he could compete with the Reverend. What if he's so good in bed she thinks I'm clumsy? He felt as though the Reverend was perched on his shoulder, grinning, daring him to be as good. Consequently, he could not get hard. He kissed her face and rubbed her breasts. Then unbuttoned her dress and moved his hands down to the triangle of hair between her thighs. All of this failed to arouse him. But Rosemary began to squirm with pleasure. Corrigan awkwardly removed his clothing. Naked, on his back, he looked like a beached albino whale. Rosemary, noticing his flaccid state, knelt and applied her lips to his penis. Corrigan moaned, closed his eyes, and pictured the Reverend pointing at him, laughing. He tried to banish the image but found it impossible not to think about something that he did not want to think about. Rosemary attempted to stimulate him with her hands. What usually worked on her husband had no effect on Corrigan. Maybe he likes kinky stuff, she thought. And moved an index finger between his massive thighs, probing for the hole behind his scrotum. When he felt her getting dangerously close to the forbidden zone, an alarm went off in his mind. His defenses rose to attention, pricking his conscience like bayonets. Shocked, he rolled away from her. Then scowled and shook his head. "A Reverend's wife!" he said with disgust. He dressed hastily and departed without another word.

Rosemary was terrified. This could be the end of her family's business. They might be evicted from the church. And what about her future coke supply?

She dressed and went to the bathroom, snorted the rest of the gram she'd started, then went to the living room and turned on the television set. About a half hour later she wondered why she couldn't feel the hazy, tingly sensation she so desperately craved.

☆ ☆ ☆

When Kevin got back to the guesthouse, Thad and Weslya were waiting for him in the parlor. They sat, sipping coffee from delicate china cups, while sitting in big armchairs with antimacassars.

"The guys who run this place are so nice!" Weslya gushed as Kevin came in. "They made us coffee while we were waiting for you."

"Yeah," Kevin agreed. "They're great. Nice place." He studied her for a moment. "You look terrific, Wes. Beautiful blouse."

"Thank you."

They finished their coffee and followed Kevin up the stairs when nobody was looking. On the way to Kevin's room, they passed a young man who had just checked in. After friendly hellos were exchanged, he watched the three of them disappear into the room at the end of the hall and shook his head in disbelief. He tried to imagine what arcane sexual couplings these three would attempt and the possibilities were too numerous to contemplate.

When the door was closed and locked behind them, Kevin sat in the chair as Thad and Weslya sprawled on the bed. It was dark outside, the room lit by the lamp on the desk.

"Well," said Thad, "I presume we had a productive day. I took particular pleasure in playing cat and mouse with the punk driving Corrigan's car. I'll bet today's a day he'll never forget for as long as he lives. What about you, Wes, were you followed?"

She looked at him and knitted her brows. "I don't think so. But I'm no expert. Maybe I was and just couldn't tell. But I had a wonderful day. I got some new clothes and walked around and saw two creepy movies. It was fun." She smiled and looked over at Kevin, ready to listen to his report.

He stretched his tired legs and crossed his arms over his chest. "My legs are killing me, but I had a good day, too. I walked a lot and saw a lot of interesting buildings — this is a great, great town. But then I got really pissed off because Sergeant Bolkonsky wasn't at the police station like he said he'd be. Nothing gets me angrier than being stood up. I wanted to talk to him and urge him to put those maniacs behind bars before they kill us. But anyway, I left the envelope and wrote a note asking him to call me here or you guys at the motel."

Thad asked, "Do you think you were followed?"

"I really couldn't say. I didn't notice anything unusual and if someone had been careful about it, I wouldn't have known. But you were, huh? I'll bet you really gave that guy the runaround."

Thad chuckled. "He's probably still looking for my car down by the waterfront."

"Good for you," said Weslya.

"One thing, Kevin," said Thad.

"What's that?"

"We still have the tape. I've got it right here." He patted the brown paper bag he'd placed on his lap.

"I don't understand." Kevin looked at him blankly.

"I substituted the tapes. The one you left is a copy of a grade Z martial arts movie. The Sergeant will get a big kick out of it."

"You mean, you used me as a decoy? Why?" Kevin tried to contain his anger. He didn't like being lied to.

"It makes perfect sense," said Thad in an appeasing tone. "Chances are that one of Corrigan's goons followed you and saw you enter with a package and leave without one. He'll tell Corrigan and Corrigan will think the police are on to him. He's bound to fuck up. Plus, we're out of danger for a while. Until Corrigan finds out we still have the tape, he won't bother us because he'll think we don't pose a threat to him anymore. Understand?"

"Yes," said Kevin sharply. "But why did you lie to me? You could have told me what was going on. I would have done it."

"That's not the point," said Thad, softly. "Maybe the motel room is bugged or something. Or maybe someone was listening at our door? By not telling you, I just made sure the plan didn't backfire."

Kevin couldn't argue with that. Still, he felt betrayed. So he tried to convince himself that Thad had acted wisely. And told himself he should admire Thad for his foresight and thoroughness. "You're a pretty smart guy," he said. "I'm sure glad we're on the same team."

"Me too," said Weslya.

"Me three," said Thad. "Frankly, I believe that together we're unbeatable. Now, here's what I propose we do next. We'll give the tape to the *Chronicle* reporter as soon as we can. If he'll listen to us and go public with this story, we'll turn everything over to the police and walk away from this entire sordid affair. Except for testifying at the trial, when that comes along."

"Good," said Weslya.

Kevin said, "I'll drink to that."

The trio left the building a few minutes later and had a leisurely dinner at a very quiet and hospitable Italian restaurant. Then Thad and Weslya drove back to the motel and Kevin returned to the guesthouse. When he arrived, he found a note under his door with a message that Jeremy had called. Kevin phoned him and they arranged to meet for a drink later that evening.

As Weslya and Thad undressed for bed, they surreptitiously eyed each other as they stripped to their underwear. When the light was off they lay in separate beds wondering what it would be like if they were together.

Chapter 15

Leona had reached the point where she had to talk to someone or burst. There was an obstacle to overcome and a lonely life to fill. But she felt that she'd spent her resources and needed help, guidance. Paulette was the ideal counselor for people with problems. Kind and wise, she generously shared herself with anyone in need. Leona knew that Paulette could help her, but she was too timid to ask. At first. But when she could no longer bear her burden unassisted, she decided it was time to talk to Paulette.

They'd met about three years before when a civic organization had formed to oust a school principal suspected of abusing children. Paulette was a teacher in the same school, Leona, a concerned citizen. When the principal had been found out and convicted, the civic group disbanded but the two women had remained close.

Paulette sat in her kitchen eating oatmeal with butter, sugar, and cinnamon. Her long, black hair, parted in the center, framed her round, open face. She wore a silver and turquoise pendant around her neck. When Leona walked in, she poured herself a cup of coffee and sat at the table opposite her friend.

"Have some oatmeal."

"I'm not hungry. Coffee's enough right now."

Paulette continued eating, content to let her friend remain silent until she felt compelled to open her heart.

Leona looked at her with love. Paulette was like a perfectly designed bridge; strong enough to bear the weight of the traffic, supple in the force of strong winds. Leona suddenly realized that the time had come for her to speak.

"I know you've been anxious to know why I came here. And I respect your restraint in not demanding an explanation from me. I'm ready to talk."

Paulette smiled at her. "I'm always ready to listen."

Leona explained to her that for the past month or so she'd been employed at the home of the man she was certain had murdered Enrique. She told her about the two men who'd been imprisoned in the basement and of the files she'd found proving Corrigan to be liar and thief. Paulette sat and listened with a serene expression. The roundness of her face, the calm of her demeanor, the size of her rotund girth, gave her the air of a feminine Buddha.

". . . and so I don't know what my next step should be and I'm worried that Corrigan is going to try and kill me because I can prove he's a criminal even though I don't know how to prove he killed my husband. And I don't know what to do with my life. I'm so lonely without Enrique. We had so many plans."

Paulette knew what her friend was going through. She, too, had lost her husband. And she'd had to fight for justice several years before when the government had tried to renege on a treaty and bulldoze her ancestors' burial grounds. Paulette was no stranger to adversity. It had taught her to fight back when necessary, to remain cool and reasonable when it was demanded, to join together with others for combined strength and power.

Paulette regarded her friend with sympathy. "You must take control. And you must stop living in the past. Your husband is gone and will never return. I know it's difficult, but you must plan your life again and start *living*. Search your heart and your mind. Go to your church and ask for your God's wisdom and guidance. I will do the same. We will talk and ask each other many questions. Perhaps, with the help of the gods, we will find some answers. I, too, am lonely. When Peter left me I thought I would die of loneliness. But I have survived. And you will too. Time is the healing force of the universe."

Leona looked at her with gratitude. Thanked her. For the first time in a long time, she felt lighter than air. She felt as though she finally had an ally. Someone to share victories and disappointments. The struggle would be easier with Paulette to help her along.

Leona fixed herself a bowl of oatmeal. She ate it and felt stronger. While washing and drying the breakfast dishes, she decided to go to church.

Dressed in a black shift with a white shawl, her hair twisted into a French knot, Leona walked into the Church of Saint Miguel on Geary Street. She'd attended Mass there with Enrique several times when they'd first arrived. But eventually they'd stopped going as their lives became more complicated and they had less time. Once Enrique had decided to run for Board of Supervisors, there'd been no time for anything except the essentials.

It was a beautiful church, dignified and elegant. Everything was cream-colored and well cared for. An aura of peaceful goodwill permeated the atmosphere and the congregation was cloaked in quiet contemplation.

Leona dipped her fingers in the holy water and offered her respects to God. Then she seated herself and prayed for guidance. The priest spoke, in a voice of quiet strength, imploring the worshipers to hold fast to their faith. A small choir sang reverently and Leona got down on her knees and prayed with a fervor she hadn't known for a long time.

When the service was over, she left and slowly walked back to Paulette's house. She asked herself what she wanted from life as she made her way up and down the hilly topography of the Mission District. The answers came to her one at a time. She wanted to avenge her husband's death. She would not rest until this was done. And at some time in the future, she would want to share her life with a man. He would never replace Enrique in her heart, but it would be better than living alone in misery. And there would be a child, for she'd wanted to have children since she was a little girl. She would love and teach her young one all of the important things that one had to know about life on earth.

For the first time since Enrique's disappearance, Leona felt in possession of a destination. A goal. She smiled inwardly. In time she would learn how to reach the place where she wanted to be and would figure out how to attain that which her heart desired.

☆ ☆ ☆

The shades were drawn in Jack Corrigan's living room. Kurt sat on the couch drinking beer. Sam sat in an armchair stroking his mustache. Corrigan twirled his glass of iced vodka and looked at his employees with steel-eyed determination.

"We've come to a crucial point in our proceedings so you'd better listen and listen well. Leona has stolen my files and no doubt plans to turn them over to the police. We've got to stop her before she does. But first we have to find her. Sam, you take the car. Kurt, you take the van."

"Where's Suzie?" Sam asked, fully aware that the question would pierce Corrigan's heart like a rusty sword.

He winced. "She and I had, er, an argument. It'll blow over."

Kurt finished the beer and crumpled the can in his hands. "The fag gave the videocassette to the Sixth Precinct. He's still at the guesthouse. The nigger and the hippie-chick are still at the motel on Market. But they were moved to a new room." Kurt giggled and looked at Sam. They hadn't told Corrigan about the fire. They'd agreed to keep quiet because he might not appreciate their foray into improvisation.

Corrigan placed his tumbler on the table, then slammed his palms together. "Shit!" I don't have enough people. We've got to keep track of those three. God only knows what they're up to now."

Sam leaned forward and fixed Corrigan with an intense stare. "Look, why don't *one* of us keep tabs on those three — they usually stick pretty close together. And the other one can look for the wetback."

"I'm giving the orders around here and you'll do what I tell you to do or else!"

"Or else what?" Sam sneered. "I could walk out right now and then where would you be? You need me, Jack. Admit it."

Corrigan smirked. "Yes, I need you. But if you walk out on me, or disobey my instructions, I'll mail a certain letter which I've been keeping locked away. I'll mail it to the police and they'll be on your tail before you can spit!"

"You can't prove anything."

"Oh, yes I can. When you first started working for me I taped that conversation we had. It has names, dates, and places regarding your former protection racket."

Sam kicked the table leg. "Shitfuck! I never knew that!"

"Now you know, you'll do as I say."

"Tape recordings are not admissible in court," said Kurt, pleased with himself for conveying this bit of information.

"What makes you a legal expert?" Corrigan harumphed. "I suggest you keep your mouth shut or you'll be looking for other work." Corrigan yawned and stretched. "You boys go to sleep now. And we'll get to work in the morning. Both of you are to look for Leona. Got that?"

"Where do we start?" asked Sam. Even if Kurt was right about tapes in court, it might put the police on his trail and it wasn't a good idea to cross someone like Jack Corrigan. Not yet, anyway.

"Good question," said Corrigan. "In the morning we'll look at her room and see if she left any clues."

Kurt asked, "What about the delivery to Mill Valley? I'm supposed to bring up a shipment tomorrow."

"That can wait. Top priority is finding Leona. Shipments will resume next week.

"I'm running low on cash for expenses," said Sam.

"I'll give you money in the morning."

A short while later, they turned out the light and went upstairs. Corrigan went into his room and closed the door. Kurt and Sam went to their bedroom which looked like it had been decorated for youngsters. There was a cowboy and Indian motif on the curtains and bedspreads, a plastic cactus lamp on the desk. Sam slept in the upper bunk of the stacked beds, Kurt below. They were both very tired and were sleeping soundly minutes after their clothing had been removed and the light extinguished.

☆ ☆ ☆

Reverend Bates took the elevator up to the eleventh floor and looked for suite number 1112. He entered and informed the receptionist that he had an appointment with Dan Greenburg. The receptionist, attracted to his handsome face and sturdy build, was slightly disappointed by his clerical collar. But she tried to hide this as she smiled and fidgeted with the intercom.

A few moments later the Reverend was ushered into Greenburg's plush office. There were abstract paintings on the walls, glass and chrome furniture, and spongy carpeting. Large windows offered a panoramic view of the downtown area and the bay.

"Reverend Bates!" Greenburg rose and met him halfway across the bright, spacious office.

"Mr. Greenburg!" They shook hands.

"Please sit." Greenburg indicated the black leather armchair as he sat in the brown leather recliner behind the desk. "I'm not one to beat around the bush, as you no doubt gathered when I came to your lovely church. I'm hoping that you've thought about my proposal and that you are favorably disposed toward it. Cigarette?" Greenburg opened a slim, golden case and held it out.

"No thank you, I don't smoke."

"Do you mind if I do?"

"Most certainly not. If God didn't want us to smoke, He wouldn't have created tobacco."

Greenburg wasn't certain if this was meant to be funny or not. The Reverend's delivery was *so* deadpan. Maybe the director would be able to do something about this. Greenburg decided to accept the statement at face value. "You know, I never thought of it that way. Good argument to use next time I'm in a roomful of non-smokers."

The Reverend smiled. Or was that a smirk. Greenburg lit a cigarette. "Anyway, Reverend, I've had some contracts prepared which I want you to look over carefully before signing." Greenburg gestured toward a file before the Reverend. "The basic stipulation is that we'll shoot one program and see how it goes. If there are no major problems we'll go ahead and shoot another five. By the time the third or fourth airs we'll know if we want to continue. At that point you'll also know if you want to continue. If all is well, we'll go on indefinitely." Greenburg looked at the silver-haired man and anxiously awaited some sort of response. He drew hard on the cigarette, then exhaled the smoke at the ceiling.

Reverend Bates picked up the file of papers and placed it on his lap. He was eager to find out how much money Greenburg was willing to pay per show. But he didn't want this eagerness to be obvious. "It all sounds very promising, Mr. Greenburg. If, through your broadcast system, I can bring the word of God to more people than I can on my own, this will all be for the good. I will go over these papers carefully and get back to you as soon as possible." He stood and extended his hand. "Thank you for taking the time to see me this morning, Mr. Greenburg."

Greenburg rose and shook his hand. "No, thank *you* for taking the time to see *me* this morning."

They smiled at one another. Then Reverend Bates, square-shouldered and brimming with confidence, walked out. On his way down in the elevator, he quickly scanned the pages to see if he could find a dollar sign. On the next to last sheet he read that the first program would yield about one thousand dollars. The next five would pay in the vicinity of two thousand dollars each.

The Reverend frowned. Not quite the goldmine he'd expected. Still, it was money and not to be dismissed.

He arrived back at the church only five minutes late for the noon service. Rosemary helped him into his gown while Billy lit the candles and hoisted the candelabra.

Chapter 16

Beneath the city, under the pavement and soil, in among the strata of igneous and sedimentary layers, threatening gases collected. Like the rising steam from a giant cauldron, these vapors gathered in pockets and lacunae beneath the bedrock, roiling, expanding, pushing to escape. When there was no more room, the gaseous atoms colliding and setting off small explosions, the ancient rock began to crumble from the pressure. Heat, smoke, cinders, and filaments of white fire rose from the underground caverns and thunderous rumbling resonated throughout the city perched above this impending upheaval. The first signs of activity could not yet be felt as Tom hurried up the stairs to his room above the chapel. Suzie, who had been secretly living there with him for two days, rose from the mattress and welcomed him with a tight embrace. She didn't mind waiting until services began, or until the Reverend and his family were asleep, to sneak down to the bathroom. Nor the greasy food that Tom brought home to her. She was glad to be free of Jack Corrigan and believed she'd found paradise with the man who bled for her.

Tom removed his clothing as Suzie slipped out of the silky bathrobe he'd bought her. They lay on the mattress rubbing each other's body, thrusting their tongues into the warmth of their wet mouths.

Suzie pulled back and gazed at him with a teasing expression. "I've been thinking," she said.

"About?"

"Trying something different."

He thought about this for a moment, afraid that she might ask him to do something repellent, anxious to find out what she wanted. "What's that?"

"You'll see," she said. Reaching for his jeans, she took the penknife from the pocket and opened it. Placing the point of the blade against the skin of his upper left arm, she made a small, clean incision, symmetrical to the one on his right arm. As the blood dribbled down his arm, she nicked herself just above her right breast. Her mouth spread into awe as the ruby red liquid made road maps on the alabaster of her torso. Over, around, and under her breast, the red lines divided and converged. "Now," she said.

Astonished and pleased, Tom slid his erection into her and started pumping.

Before either of them could climax, a fissure in the crust below erupted and rocked the hills and valleys, the streets and homes. Suzie and Tom, in tune with these vibrations, felt that they were about to experience the most profound orgasm they would ever know.

One floor below, Billy turned his face from the television screen and said, "Earthquake," in a matter-of-fact tone. There were thudding sounds coming from Tom's room above, and the building shook like it was under attack.

"So it would appear," said his father, returning to his magazine.

"Don't worry, baby, happens all the time," said Rosemary as she got to her feet and headed for the bathroom. It seemed lately that no matter how much brain tabasco she snorted, it didn't work like it used to. Still, she kept trying, hoping that blessed relief would come.

Below, the candelabra dangling from the ceiling of the chapel swayed like a hastily abandoned swing in a playground. In the buildings jutting from the sides of the hills, floors shook, chandeliers swayed, bibelots fell and shattered. Like an electric current racing along a network of wire, the tremors reached to the extremities in spiraling waves. The city became taut and uncertain, like a man juggling hand grenades on a plank over a barrel.

"It felt like an atomic bomb fell nearby," said Kevin, his arms wrapped around Jeremy's hard, glistening body.

"Earthquake," said Jeremy, running his tongue inside the groove of Kevin's right ear.

"Aren't we supposed to stand in a doorway or something?"

"If we're gonna die, we're gonna die. Shut up and kiss me again," said Jeremy. He stiffened his tongue and probed the back of Kevin's throat. Kevin felt a second stirring in his groin, a renewed surge of power from the rising sap.

The bridges spanning the bay breathed with the impact of shifting bedrock, tempestuous waters, and brittle, merciless winds. Like synapses shooting smoke signals over the water, the bridges communicated the impulses, up and down, back and forth. Land masses and bodies of water, streets and sidewalks, all retained their general shapes while swelling slightly here, retreating a bit there. Electrons and neutrons, protons and quarks, sped up, pushing each other faster with orbits growing oblate. Movement and velocity altered; patterns and functions remained.

In the bed near the window of the motel room, Thad and Weslya were oblivious to the faster action, the brighter lights, the louder bells of the city-turned-pinball machine. They writhed and struggled on the damp sheets, their bodies aching for one another. Weslya arched her spine to meet Thad's powerful, swingy thrusts, their senses too busy keeping track of their own chemistry to register the changes all around. The environment was transformed. Windows breathed slightly, walls jumped as though tickled by cold fingers. But the bed bounced and fishtailed like a stock car, steaming molten rubber where the tires meet the road.

Kurt, in the white van, Sam, in the red car, felt their vehicles vibrate as the roads carried the impact of cracking asphalt across the city, over the bridges, out past the turbulent waters. As they searched for the traitor who had absconded with the secret files of their master and protector, they were barely aware of the tumult and frenzy going on inside of the city's many buildings. As children cried and adults tried to save valuables, and protect themselves from falling plaster, drivers felt the roads shimmy, their vehicles swerve, but these minor ripples came and went, eventually disappearing altogether.

Kurt believed that earthquakes were fun, something to relieve the monotony of existence. They were an occasion for allowing yourself to be scared, knowing that everything was going to turn out all right. Like going to a monster movie, you could abandon yourself to the tingling sensation of disaster because when it was over life would resume its familiar patterns.

To Sam, earthquakes were simply a nuisance to be endured like red lights, policemen, and ugly women. He tolerated these lapses like the pits of olives which must be spit out before you could swallow the tangy meat. Gritting his teeth and cursing out loud, he regarded the trembling earth as an obstacle course which must be defeated before you could reach the goal line and score points. As though being chased by burly tackles whose only thought was to bring him down, Sam clutched the steering wheel, kept his left foot hovering over the brake and felt, with his right heel, the vibrations of the pavement below.

While many slept and simply bobbed up and down like buoys in treacherous waters, others felt adrenaline racing, hearts pounding, sweat pouring forth in fits of anxiety, fear, desperation. For every lamb asleep in a warm, fleecy bed, there was a jackal shrieking to the heavens as though the very firmament had been pulled away and there was nothing between your feet and the cold, hard earth but light and air. So insubstantial, it couldn't protect you from anything, but would let you drop until your bones splintered on jagged rocks, your blood spilling from broken veins and running in rivulets to the parched earth where it would filter down, into the incendiary cauldron where all the trouble began.

Corrigan ran up to his roof at the first tremor and looked out over the dark city. He expected to see mobs of people fleeing in distress as though chased by a carnivorous beast, hungry from centuries of starvation. But there was no panic, no dread, just the same city embedded in hillsides with tiny lights flickering. Beneath his feet, the solid building in which he lived felt like a cube of Jello. Corrigan ran down the stairs and jumped into his bed, pulling the blanket over his face. He wanted to run downstairs and get a bottle of vodka, bring it to bed, and drink himself into a stupor. But he was too frightened to leave his bed.

There were fires starting all over the city from broken gas pipes, unattended ovens, smoldering cigarette butts lying in ashtrays. A hundred alarms sounded and sirens screeched in the night. Drexel Johnson and Erika Hong led a brigade of firewomen who rescued people trapped in crumbling buildings, drove accident victims to various hospitals, found shelters for the newly homeless. It took oceans of water to extinguish the many flames of destruction scattered throughout the metropolitan area.

In the kitchen of Paulette's house, she and Leona drank herbal tea and felt the earth beneath them undulate like a dancer seduced by fast music. They talked and comforted one another. Both had been through many earthquakes and were aware that there was usually little damage, but the possibility for catastrophe could not be dismissed. They talked about movies they wanted to see. Leona told Paulette about a book of poetry she'd just read. Paulette told her anecdotes about her students; how sometimes they were so bright and charming, how at other times they disappointed her with their pettiness and mean ways. It was only for a minute or two that Paulette's house felt like an ice cube in a virulent sea. Then there were brief, decreasingly scary aftershocks for a couple of hours. Eventually all was silent and still. After one more cup of tea, they went to sleep. As Paulette turned back the blanket on her bed, she thanked the good spirits for quelling the planet's angry mood. As Leona tucked in the sheets on the couch in Paulette's living room, she prayed to God to protect and guide her. Then whispered good night to Enrique who she knew was somewhere in the Kingdom of Heaven, watching over her, protecting her from the evil forces of the world.

Chapter 17

In the morning, mist rose from the ground, revealing the scattered debris, the shards of destruction from the previous night's bitter outburst. Broken glass and wind-swept trash littered the streets and sidewalks. Charred, damp timber was all that remained of some older houses; here and there wisps of smoke floated into the sky and disappeared. There were a few banged-up cars and crumpled sign posts. But as the sun melted the cool haze of daybreak, the city awoke and resumed its motion. Detritus was cleared, repairs began, and progress continued.

When Thad woke up, the first thing he did was call Delia, his girlfriend. Weslya was still sleeping when he lifted the receiver and dialed.

"Hello?"

"Delia, this is Thad."

"Oh, really? How nice for you."

"Come on, don't give me a hard time. I apologize."

"Oh, Lord, he apologizes! Well, then I guess everything's okay."

"Look, I ran into some trouble. The reason I didn't show up that night was because I was chained to a pole in some asshole's basement."

"Right. The check's in the mail and I promise I won't come in your mouth. Look. I'm tired of waiting around for you to show up and apologize. As far as I'm concerned, we're through. You hear me talkin' to ya? Don't call. Don't write. Stay away."

When the connection broke, Thad's ear recoiled from the loud thwack. He slammed his receiver down, then immediately regretted it as Weslya moaned and opened her eyes.

"Didn't mean to wake you, go back to sleep."

Weslya took in his naked splendor and smiled as the previous evening's events gathered in her consciousness. "Good morning."

He crawled into the bed, snuggling alongside her. "Go back to sleep," he whispered. As Weslya slid back into slumber, Thad held her in his arms. It was definitely over with Delia. He'd taken advantage of her sweet nature too many times. She said it was over and she meant it. And now there was a new complication. Weslya. She was dynamite in bed. But would they be happy together within the confines of a formal relationship? Would she want to have a relationship? Maybe she just liked having sex.

As she breathed gently in a calm, easy rhythm, Thad disengaged himself and went to the bathroom. After brushing his teeth, he showered, scrubbing his body with a washcloth and soap. He hummed an old blues tune: "You Don't Miss Your Water ('Til Your Well Runs Dry)."

Weslya woke up while Thad showered. Wow, it had been sensational the night before. Thad was a terrific lover: sensitive, giving, not too rough. Weslya, who had been denying the pull of her sexuality for so long, suddenly found herself wanting more of it and often. She hoped Thad would be willing to play again, as long as it didn't create obligations, declarations, and intentions. Promises made under the influence of sex were usually broken. It's best to deal with sex as a thing unto itself and not burden it with weight that might make it drown.

After Thad emerged from the bathroom, Weslya entered. She washed her hair, soaped herself with her hands, and enjoyed every sensation as the warm, hard-hitting water massaged her.

When she was dressed, she sat on the bed looking at Thad. He waited to see if she would say anything about last night. She was silent. Nothing would be said unless he spoke first. He didn't feel like saying anything. Why soil a situation which, so far, was immaculate?

"Hungry?" he finally asked. "Me, I'm starved."

"Yes, I am too."

He looked at his wristwatch. It was almost ten-thirty. "Breakfast, brunch, or lunch?"

"Doesn't matter," she said, "Anything."

Just then, there was a knock on the door.

Thad motioned for Weslya to duck. She dropped to her hands and knees on the carpet between the beds. Thad cautiously looked through the slit in the curtains, prepared to move fast. He sighed. "Relax. It's only Kevin and a friend of his, I presume."

Thad opened the door. "Good morning," he beamed with joviality.

"Morning," said Kevin, walking in. "I'd like you to meet my friend, Jeremy. Jeremy, this is Thad."

The two men shook hands.

Weslya stepped forward. When his face emerged from the shadows, she shrieked, "JEREMY! What are you doing here?"

"I see you've already met," said Kevin.

"Weslya, what are *you* doing here?"

Thad looked at Kevin; Kevin looked at Thad.

Weslya's brain began to spin like the label on a 45 rpm single. Part of her was happy to see Jeremy—she was glad he was alive and well. But another part of her felt angry. She didn't need the turmoil of the bitter memories, the pain of cauterized wounds reopening.

Jeremy moved toward her with his arms outstretched. She stepped back. With a blank, almost cool expression she said, "You're looking well. Nice to see you again."

"Gosh, it's great to see you again too, you're looking terrific."

"Thank you." She looked at Thad and Kevin hoping one of them would suggest something that might smooth this awkward confrontation. They looked at her inquiringly.

"I guess you're still pretty upset, huh, Wes?" Jeremy looked crushed.

"Shit! Upset isn't the word for it. Just when I thought I might be able to forget about you forever, here you are to remind me how betrayed—no, make that pissed off—I felt when you left."

"But, Wes, I thought we'd settled all this—I thought you understood that I really had no choice . . ."

She turned to Thad and Kevin. "It's about time for breakfast, I think."

"Good idea," said Thad.

They moved out the door. Thad locked it. He and Weslya walked together, a few yards ahead of Jeremy and Kevin.

Jeremy whispered, "I didn't mean to get her so upset." Kevin looked at him, concerned, but didn't know what to say. They arrived at Lucretia's, several blocks away. The menu featured fifty different types of omelettes, French toast, pancakes, sausages, bacon, and over twenty-five varieties of baked goods from corn muffins to fruit-filled croissants.

The coffee, strong and aromatic, had not a trace of bitterness. As the four ate, Thad tried to start various conversational courses that would not lead to controversy or contention. Weslya stared into space, tight-lipped. Jeremy looked at his plate, embarrassed. Kevin decided he had to try to melt this cold spell.

"C'mon, Wes, Jeremy said he's sorry."

"A few words can't make up for all the misery."

"I made a mistake. I admit it. I apologize. I wish I'd had the guts to face up to my true nature before I met you. But I was too scared. When we met I thought we were going to spend the rest of our lives together in that little cabin on the hill. Growing our own vegetables and stuff. And then, eventually, I realized that I was living a lie and had to get out. I never meant to hurt you."

Weslya looked away, signalled the waiter for more coffee.

"Won't you even talk to me?" he pleaded.

"The only thing on my mind right now," she informed him, "is this little adventure with Thad and Kevin."

"What little adventure?"

Kevin broke in. "That's what I was going to tell you about after you met these people, because I didn't think you'd believe me without the word of two other witnesses." Kevin hoped that this change of subject would alleviate the tension.

As the breadbaskets emptied and the other food disappeared, Thad informed Jeremy of all that had happened prior to his meeting Kevin, who brought the story up to the part of meeting Weslya, who related, rather icily, everything that had occurred up to the point where Thad fooled Corrigan into thinking the police had the videocassette.

"What are we going to do now?" Jeremy asked.

"We?" hissed Weslya.

"I'd like to help if I can," he said.

"You're welcome as far as I'm concerned," said Thad.

"Me, too," Kevin agreed.

Weslya was not thrilled at this prospect, but couldn't find any sound objections. She remained silent and expressionless.

"The next step," said Thad, "is to get the cassette to the reporter at the *Chronicle*."

While Kevin and Thad fought over who would pay for the check, Jeremy stared wistfully across the table. Weslya refused to acknowledge his gaze. He thought of fighting side by side with her in the struggle to liberate People's Park. She recalled the sun-soaked afternoons of wild, naked sex on the mountainside.

Kevin and Thad finally decided to split the bill because each claimed it was his turn to pay and neither would yield a centimeter of ground.

☆ ☆ ☆

Leona entered the police station clutching a large envelope with a fold-down clasp. After passing through the metal detector, she introduced herself to the officer behind the desk and informed him that she had an appointment with Sergeant Bolkonsky. The officer paged the Sergeant, who arrived at the desk a few minutes later.

"Sorry it took me so long," he apologized, "but we've had quite a few problems dealing with the mess from the earthquake last night. Let's go to my cubicle and talk," he said, leading her down a long hallway with chipped paint on the walls and fluorescent lights overhead.

Sergeant Andrew Bolkonsky was a handsome man with a ruddy complexion, cornflower blue eyes, and closely cropped black hair. His upper body was well developed, he had a slim waist, and was slightly bowlegged.

Leona breathed in his maleness as he ushered her into a tiny, sectioned-off makeshift office within a warren of acoustical tile dividers. They sat on folding chairs so close to one another their knees touched.

Leona laid her package on her lap and waited for the sergeant to begin. After rearranging a few piles of forms on the desk, he looked at her and asked, "You said this was in reference to . . .?"

"Jack Corrigan."

He looked at her with amusement. "The other day someone left me a videotape claiming that it proved a certain Jack Corrigan murdered a Board of Supervisors candidate, but the video was a cheap kung-fu movie." He smiled.

Leona looked at him with stark solemnity. "Corrigan *did* murder a candidate who just happened to be my husband. I don't know who would have a tape that could prove it."

"The guy's name is . . ." he looked through a pile of papers and lifted one out, ". . . Thaddeus Heath and someone else named Kevin Conover."

Leona wondered if these were the names of the guys whom she'd helped escape. "Anyway," she said, "I *can* prove that Corrigan's a thief with the file I brought. I thought that if we can't get him for the murder, we can get him for theft and fraud."

"How did you get the files?"

"I stole them."

He shook his head. "You should have filed a complaint first and we would have taken it from there."

Leona started to cry. It seemed that every time she was beginning to make some progress her plans were thwarted.

The sergeant pulled a pressed handkerchief from the rear pocket of his uniform and gave it to her. She wiped the corners of her eyes and then blew her nose. "I'm sorry," she sniffed. "I don't usually break down like this."

"It's all right." He had such a kind smile. "I assure you I will do everything I can to help you solve your problem. Okay?"

"Yes, thank you," she said, feeling a bit more in control.

"Now why don't you fill out these forms . . ." he handed her a sheaf of papers and a ball point pen with teeth marks on the handle, ". . . and let me have a look at what you brought."

She handed him the envelope and started filling out the forms. He opened it and began reading.

When she finished supplying all of the requested information, Leona put the pen on the desk and sighed. The sergeant was engrossed in the ledgers she'd given him. She watched him read, waiting expectantly.

He sensed her staring at him and looked up, embarrassed. "Sorry. I guess I got a little carried away. Leave this stuff with me and I'll get back to you in a day or so."

"Thank you," she said.

He walked her to the front door and shook her hand. "Don't you worry, Mrs. Ramirez. I'll do everything I can."

Leona left the building and walked back to Paulette's house. She couldn't get the image of Sergeant Bolkonsky's face out of her mind. It had such strength and sincerity. He exuded an air of confidence and good humor which excited her. As anxious as she was to hear from him regarding her case, she was even more interested in further communication because he had made such a favorable impression.

Chapter 18

It was almost time for the noon service. In the turmoil of the previous evening, the floor of the church had become spackled with plaster chips. A few of the pews had become misaligned and several candles had fallen from the candelabra.

As Billy and Rosemary swept and scooped, the Reverend paced in the anteroom, glancing at his wristwatch. The service was to begin in less than five minutes and Tom had not yet appeared. He was usually seated in the moldy green chair at least fifteen minutes prior to the commencement. A being of predictable habits, Tom made himself conspicuous by improvising.

When the floor was clean and the pews rearranged, the candelabra was lowered and each empty sconce received a new, white taper. After Billy hoisted it back into place, he went to the anteroom to don his altar boy costume.

His father asked, "Have you seen Tom?"

"No," he replied and slipped his head through the opening in the white silk. The Reverend glanced at his wife with a questioning look. Rosemary placed her hand at her throat. "I haven't seem him either."

The Reverend resumed pacing. "He's never been late before."

"Maybe he overslept," said Rosemary. "Honey," she said to the boy, "will you run upstairs and see if Tom is in his room?"

"Okay." He left and crossed the stage. The pews were beginning to fill up with people. Young and old, black and white, male and female. All sorts.

Billy ran up the first flight of stairs, raced across the landing, then took the second flight two steps at a time. Panting, he knocked on the door opposite the attic. Nothing could be heard from within the room.

Billy sensed that something was wrong. His feet felt funny. When he looked down, he saw that the floor was wet. With the indirect lighting from the floor below, it looked like a puddle of black water. It was seeping from the other side of the closed door.

He knocked again. Then waited. Still no response. With extreme caution, he slowly opened the door. His heart pounded against his ribcage and he felt tingly all over. By the light coming through the window he could see the fallen beams, the mangled bodies, and dull red spattered all over the mattress and floor.

He screamed. His voice flew from his throat as though he'd been caught in a steel trap. He stood there, staring at the open-eyed corpses, stark naked, crushed. He recognized Tom, noticed all of the scars all over his body, and the Asian woman beneath him who came to pick up the money.

Billy finally managed to pull himself from the spectacle. Running down the stairs he collided with his parents on the landing, who'd rushed up when they heard him scream.

Billy pointed upwards and looked at them, his face a study in naked terror. Rosemary knelt and held his shoulders. "Honey, what is it?" she asked, nervously.

"Up there," he pointed.

"What's up there, son?" The Reverend's forehead wrinkled with concern.

"Tom and the money lady. The ceiling fell on them."

"Oh, my God," gasped Rosemary.

The Reverend ran up the stairs and looked through the door. After surveying the room, he cursed under his breath, closed the door, and shook his head in anger. On his way down the stairs, his mind raced to keep up with these unexpected obstacles. What would he tell his congregation? It took him a second to decide that he'd tell them Tom had been called home to tend his ailing mother. That ought to hold them. Then he'd have to start looking for some other attraction to fill the church. It would be best not to tell the television people that the star of the show was dead. They might decide to cancel the program. And that was unthinkable. The show must go on. The money must keep rolling in.

☆ ☆ ☆

As Leona made her way through the maze of shadowy hills she thought about the attractive policeman she'd just met. There was nothing she could do to bring Enrique back and she did not want to spend the rest of her life alone. She couldn't stay with Paulette forever; she had to make a new life for herself.

105

Once Corrigan was brought to justice, she'd start over: find a job, fall in love, get a nice apartment.

As she turned off Van Ness, Sam spotted her. He was braked at a red light. When he saw her walk right into his field of vision, he rejoiced. Then he lowered his face so she wouldn't recognize him. As soon as she was far enough away from him, he followed her discreetly.

Sam wanted very much to seize this opportune situation and exact his own personal revenge for stealing the boss's files. He imagined running her down, beating her up, shooting her, or slicing her open like a juicy tomato. But he held these impulses in check when a tiny voice at the back of his brain reminded him that Corrigan might fire him if he didn't obey his instructions.

Reining himself in like a lassoed stallion, he slowly paced Leona up, down, and around until she entered a small, white clapboard house. After memorizing the address, he headed back to Corrigan's house to claim credit for having found the traitor. Perhaps Corrigan would reward him by allowing him to mete out the punishment in any way he pleased. He smiled and increased the volume of the cassette player on the passenger seat.

☆ ☆ ☆

On the way to the building that housed the staff and offices of the *Chronicle*, Thad told Jeremy all about his background as an activist in the anti-war and civil rights movements. Jeremy hung on every word, fascinated by Thad's first-person accounts of marches, riots, demonstrations, and consciousness-raising groups. Weslya sat up front next to Thad. Kevin and Jeremy were in the back. As Thad maneuvered the car through the crowded streets, Kevin grew bored listening to all the talk about Thad's past. He reached for Thad's Walkman, on the armrest between the front seats. The cassette within had no label.

Kevin interrupted, "What's on this tape?"

"It's a tape I made myself. Assorted blues and jazz cuts."

"Sounds good," said Kevin, putting the headphones in place, pressing the play button. The first tune was a big band number with growly trombones and jungle rhythms. Kevin guessed that it was Duke Ellington and his Orchestra. The second song was a weird blues thing sung by what sounded like an older black man accompanying himself on guitar. When Kevin heard the lyrics he was mortified. The song was about beating up a girlfriend because she was so stupid. Kevin pulled the headphones off and pressed the stop button. Thad was now relating his experiences in Vietnam.

"What the fuck is this shit?" Kevin interrupted.

"Huh?" said Thad.

"This song—something about smacking his girlfriend with a wooden plank. What kind of crap is that?"

"Oh, I see," said Thad, keeping his eyes on the traffic. "That song is an artifact from the past. Before men had any idea about women's rights or feminism."

"How can you listen to it?" Kevin glowered. "It's sexist bullshit, downright insulting. It promotes violence against women."

Thad made a sharp right turn and the passengers swayed to the side, then uprighted themselves. "When I listen to music like that, it's with the understanding that it's from a different place and time and that these artists did not have access to the kind of education that I did so I allow that there might be a certain ignorance—or shall I say naivete—that I take into account."

"He's right," said Jeremy. "We can't expect the past to conform to modern standards. There's sexism in Shakespeare's plays but they're still performed."

"That's true," said Kevin. "Still, hearing that song is unsettling. I guess because it reminds me that even though certain people are aware of sexism and racism, a lot of people are still guilty of it."

Weslya didn't say anything. It seemed pointless. Men just couldn't seem to grasp that womanhood is not something to be argued about. Just accepted and respected. Like manhood. But men — most of them, anyway — whether straight or gay, black or white, were usually just . . . boys.

Just then, Thad chortled and gunned the car into second gear. "What are you doing?" gasped Weslya, clutching the dashboard with both hands.

Thad shouted, "There goes that thug of Corrigan's. Let's put the fear of God into his soul."

The car leaped forward like a bullet. The passengers held onto whatever their hands could grasp.

Thad tapped bumpers and Sam, after regaining his equilibrium, looked at his rearview. "SHITFUCK!" he shouted and stepped on the gas. The car roared down the street, recklessly dodging other vehicles and pedestrians, weaving through the dense traffic.

"I hope all of your seatbelts are fastened," said Thad as the car lurched into pursuit.

Sam wound his car through narrow streets and got in line for the bridge to Oakland. Thad and passengers were three cars behind.

"Who's this guy?" Jeremy asked.

"One of Corrigan's henchmen," said Kevin.

"The bastard set our hotel room on fire," said Weslya.

"We don't know that for certain," said Thad.

As the late afternoon traffic slowly crawled across the bridge, the sun began casting longer shadows across the hills and valleys. When Sam drove down off the exit ramp, he turned and sped toward Berkeley. Thad swerved around a pick-up truck and stayed right on his tail. Occasionally he would goose the engine and tap bumpers. Sam would grit his teeth and growl.

They raced through the streets of Berkeley, verdant and stately, with manicured lawns and imitation Greek buildings on either side. Students, arms laden with books, ambled along, startled by the speeding cars.

"This place sure has changed," said Weslya, noting the students' clothing and hairstyles.

"Sure has," said Jeremy. "I remember when this place looked like a carnival of the bizarre. Now it looks like a shopping mall."

"What about the reporter at the *Chronicle*?" asked Kevin.

"He might still be there this evening," said Thad, making a sharp left. "If not, we'll drop the cassette off tomorrow."

Sam flew down the center of town, scattering men, women, and children in his wake. Fortunately, no one was harmed. Thad stayed with him, following the trail that led back to the bridge. When they hit the downtown area, Sam drove to Corrigan's house. Thad let him get away and drove to the newspaper building.

☆ ☆ ☆

Kurt had been following Thad's car in the van, not particularly paying too much attention; merely going forward when required, hanging back when necessary. His mind was on other things. Like, when was the real action going to start? All of this surveillance and driving around didn't appeal to him at all. He wanted pistols to fire, arrows to fly, cannons to roar, bombs to fall.

He was supposed to be looking for Leona. But when Thad's car went by him, Kurt shifted and took off. He couldn't see that Sam's car was just ahead of Thad's. But thinking that he

108

might finally see some action, Kurt threw his attention toward following the enemy vehicle.

As the van crawled along the bottle-necked bridge, Kurt was overwhelmed with anxiety. He didn't have the patience for traffic jams. He wanted to move fast, feel the van flying like a bombardier in a jet. He honked his horn repeatedly but the cars in front hardly moved at all.

Just as the van was leaving the exit ramp, the left rear tire blew out. Kurt slammed his palm against the steering wheel and reluctantly pulled the van off the road to change the tire.

By the time he finished and was back behind the wheel, the enemy was nowhere in sight.

Kurt sucked down his pride, crossed back over the bridge, and drove to Corrigan's. He dreaded telling the boss what had happened. He'd be punished for sure. But bad soldiers always wound up in the brig. He accepted this inevitability because in every movie he'd ever seen, the heroes always accepted their failures with solemn dignity. They took it like real men. And so would Kurt.

Chapter 19

There were wires and cables tendriling everywhere — under, over and around the pews — from the television cameras to the mobil TV unit parked outside the church. Technicians with tools dangling from utility belts communicated via walkie-talkie as they made connections, positioned cameras, tested lights and microphones.

Reverend Bates sat in the anteroom with his wife and son as a makeup artist pancaked their foreheads, darkened their eyebrows, and reddened their cheeks. Rosemary sniffled, one of the symptoms of her withdrawal. She'd been forced to endure the chills, vomiting, and cramps in silence because she could not tell her husband or her son she'd become hooked on an illegal substance.

The Reverend was sweating like a wedge of cheese in the sun. He still hadn't decided what to do about the mess upstairs. But he knew something had to done very soon. The odor was beginning to spread.

Billy sat there, fidgety with nervous energy because he was going to be on television — easily the most important occasion so far in his young life.

When the makeup artist was finished, she left the room.

A few moments later Dan Greenburg entered. "Remember now, this is just a rehearsal so don't be nervous. No one will ever see this except us."

This disappointed Billy. He didn't know what a rehearsal was and thought that this performance was to be broadcast. He felt very let down, but at least he now knew what the word rehearsal meant — not for real.

Greenburg lit a cigarette. "Where's Tom Slater? He's the star of the show, you know. Without him, this'll never fly."

Rosemary turned to Billy and gave him the look that said, keep your mouth shut.

110

"Well, Dan, you see," said Reverend Bates, "he wasn't feeling too well and we thought it would be best if he rested up so he'd be in tip-top shape for the first real show."

"I see. Well, tell him for me that we all wish him a speedy recovery."

"I will."

"And Mrs. Bates. You should be taking care of that cold."

"I am, Mr. Greenburg, but it's a real pip."

"Call me Dan."

"Call me Rosemary."

Greenburg glanced at his wristwatch. "Well, I've got to go to the truck now. We'll be starting in less than two minutes. Good luck!"

"Thank you," they chorused.

The Reverend fixed his wife and son with a cold glare. "Remember, don't fuck anything up. Play it just like we planned. If either of you screws up, I swear I'll kill you."

☆ ☆ ☆

Thad and Kevin had dinner with Vince Pileggi at an elegant restaurant, La Ronde, known for its fine table linens, crystal goblets and dazzling chandeliers.

Thad wore his jeans, a button-down shirt, and a sports jacket. Kevin had put on a Machado silk jacket with a Shikoko shirt and gabardine slacks. Vince inhabited a rumpled brown suit, at least two sizes too large.

As the waiter dipped to serve the appetizers, the reporter sipped his gin and began talking. "I saw the video you left for me last night. Pretty convincing. The part where Corrigan is telling those two guys he'll turn them in to immigration was kind of scary. And the other part, with Ramirez predicting his own death gave me the creeps."

Pileggi looked at Kevin, expecting a response. "I haven't seen it," Kevin confessed. "I only know what I've been through — which is enough to convince me that Corrigan is capable of anything."

"How did you get hold of it?" Vince turned to Thad.

"I used to work at Corrigan's bar, Sutter's Mill, and I overheard enough stuff so I was able to figure out he was up to no good. Then one day, Enrique Ramirez stopped in because he was investigating Corrigan. We started talking and pooled our information. When he started to think that something might happen to him, he finished the tape and gave it to me. He disappeared a few days later."

111

Vince Pileggi sat back from his calamari and put down his fork. He had a long, thin face, dark coloring, and intense eyes. When he talked, his upper lip curled into a sneer. "There have been rumors circulating that Corrigan's responsible for a lot of other stuff as well. They say he deals bad dope and has a mail fraud racket. Not to mention his suspicious connection with the Church of Divine Forgiveness."

"What's that?" asked Thad.

"One of those churches for the gullible poor where the preacher crowbars them from the little money they have."

"What can we do?" asked Kevin.

"Do you think the police should see the video?" Thad asked.

"First," said Vince, "let me do some digging, see if I can put some of my research people on this. I'll write a story — see if there's any response. Some witnesses may come forward."

"And what should we do?" Kevin asked again.

"Stay out of Corrigan's way and sit tight."

The meal continued and the talk turned to other things. Kevin and Thad told Pileggi about themselves. Pileggi filled them in on some evidence he'd uncovered involving federal agents entrapping mail-order pornography purchasers.

When the meal was over, they left the restaurant and shook hands. Pileggi returned to his car and drove away.

Thad and Kevin walked leisurely, digesting their meal. They talked about Weslya and Jeremy and the coincidence of them meeting under such odd circumstances. Two young men passed them on the sidewalk. One of them — wearing a baseball jacket, said, "Faggots! Too many of 'em 'round here. Wish they'd all die already."

The other, heavier, wearing a green sweatshirt, agreed.

Kevin shoved his hands in his pants pocket. His shoulders stiffened and he walked on. Thad grabbed his arm. "Aren't you going to do anything?"

"Like what?"

"Oh, I don't know," said Thad. "Like kick 'em in the nuts, smash their faces. Something."

"What good would it do?"

"Make me feel better."

Kevin didn't know what to say at first. Then thought of, "Violence only breeds more violence."

Thad turned and started running after the two guys. Kevin followed. When they realized they were being chased, the two guys started to run. As they approached Fisherman's Wharf, they leapt up the stairs to Ghirardelli Plaza. Multi-levels of shops with flagstone patios, staircases, and balconies provided a three-story labyrinth to get lost in. As their feet pounded on the tiles of the mall, they raced away from their pursuers with mounting fear.

At this point, Thad was eager to lash out at anyone who got in his way. And he figured Kevin needed some consciousness-raising when it came to the subject of fighting back.

As Kevin bounded up the stairs after Thad, he felt a surge of power. He'd been insulted before but had never retaliated. It felt good to be taking action.

On the second tier, the guy in the green sweatshirt glanced over the wrought-iron railing and saw that Thad and Kevin were closing the gap. His feet churned faster, trying to get away.

Thad leapt up the staircase with Kevin right behind him. The guy in the green sweatshirt shot forward, but Thad managed to grab the one in the baseball jacket. He jerked him back by the collar, spun him around, and connected his fist with the other's jaw. He fell to the ground, moaning, clutching his face.

The one in the green sweatshirt hesitated for a moment, wondering if he should go back to help his friend. This gave Kevin the time to catch up with him. Kevin yanked his hair and flung him to the ground, then lifted him by his arm, drew back his fist, and punched the guy's face with all the force he'd built up during the years of walking away. "Yeow!" he yelled, as Kevin's knuckles made contact. The guy in the sweatshirt crumpled to the ground, clutching his jaw. Kevin shook his hand and winced, rubbing the sore knuckles of his right hand.

Thad spat on the ground, put his arm around Kevin's shoulder, and steered him away. "That's what I would do if I was gay and someone called me a faggot," Thad grinned.

"If I stopped to fight every time someone insulted me," said Kevin, "I wouldn't have time for anything else."

"Sometimes that's what it takes."

"I have to admit it felt good at first. But I hope I never have to do this again. I'm really a very nonviolent person."

Thad chuckled. "Oh yeah? Try convincing that bloody mess crawling around looking for his teeth back there." He patted Kevin's back and they slowly walked away from the scene of their encounter.

Chapter 20

Corrigan's eyes were silvery pink and looked like they might pop out of his face. As his complexion reddened, he downed a jigger of vodka and wiped his lips with the cuff of his sleeve.

"Something's got to give, boys. We've reached a crucial stage in our proceedings. What we do in the next few days will decide our fates forever!"

Kurt and Sam looked at him in disbelief. He was ranting like a madman. Had his mind snapped, or was he a true visionary who had seen a glimpse of the future?"

"Why, you boys have been like sons to me. And I need to know if you're with me or against me."

"With you," said Kurt in desperation, his boyish face betraying his eagerness to believe in something and someone.

"Me too," said Sam, all nonchalance.

"Line 'em up, Joe!" Corrigan shouted, and the bartender came over with a bottle of Absolut. He filled the three shot glass in a row on the bar and quickly moved back to the other end. It was early evening and the after-work crowd had packed Sutter's Mill. Businessmen in three-piece suits, secretaries in tasteful skirts and blouses, and bar girls in cheap, tight dresses, crushed against one another vying for the bartender's attention. Corrigan, Kurt, and Sam sat at the bar, squeezed together by the pressing bodies.

"Here's where we stand," said Corrigan, trying to organize his thoughts. "Suzie's left us and Leona's a traitor. She'll have to be dealt with. Now that we know her address it should be easy. Our candy man has fucked up and ruined my reputation. The cops have the videotape and I still haven't figured out how that faggot fits into all of this."

"What about the hippie chick?" asked Kurt.

"And the faggot's boyfriend?" added Sam. "How do they fit in?"

114

"I don't know for sure," Corrigan confessed. "But it's clear who our enemies are and who our friends are. And tomorrow is the big day. Everything could change drastically tomorrow. It's the first taping for the TV show at the church. We all have to be there. We have to clap and scream and let the producers know that his show is going to be a hit! If it takes off like I'm hoping it will, we'll start opening churches from Seattle to Bangor. And then we won't have to worry about all of the other stuff. We'll leave town, set up operations somewhere else, and sit back while the money dances into our hands."

"Sounds good," said Kurt, all earnestness.

"Yeah," said Sam, finishing his vodka, signalling Joe for a refill.

☆ ☆ ☆

When Jeremy finished telling Kevin how upset he was over Weslya's refusal to forgive him, Kevin told him what the reporter had said the previous evening. ". . . so evidently, they've been keeping tabs on Corrigan all along and there's some big to-do at this rip-off church this evening and Thad suggested that we should all be there."

When they finished eating, they left the restaurant and kissed on the sidewalk. "Remember," said Kevin, "six o'clock at the church."

"I'll be there, it'll be interesting," said Jeremy.

They embraced. Jeremy seized Kevin's hand and squeezed it.

"What did you do to your hand?" Jeremy asked.

Kevin palmed his raw knuckles, "Nothing. Just scraped it, that's all."

"You should cover it so it doesn't get infected."

"I will."

Kevin walked back to the guesthouse. Whenever he thought about this weird church that Pileggi had told him and Thad about, he got a little nervous. His stomach felt like he'd swallowed a burning chunk of coal. He hated those television churches with terrorist preachers. And the thought of someone making himself bleed for money, that was too abhorrent to even think about.

Still, it was possible that the church service that evening could be the end of Kevin's troubles — insofar as Jack Corrigan was concerned.

The other problem was back in New York. Bryan. It had

been over two weeks since they'd spoken. Bryan would be angry that Kevin hadn't called sooner.

And then, of course, there was Jeremy. Kevin hadn't planned on getting romantically involved while vacationing, but he couldn't ignore the stirrings in his heart.

He entered the guesthouse and walked up to his room. Looked at his wristwatch and dialed. It would be morning in New York. Bryan would be practicing his scales.

"Hello?"

"Bryan, it's Kevin."

"Kevin! I've missed you. Why didn't you call?"

"Well, you see, it's like this . . ." and Kevin told him everything that had happened since waking up in Corrigan's basement to having dinner with Vince Pileggi the night before. ". . . and what they said couldn't be done has finally occurred with a vengeance."

"If what you're about to tell me is as far-fetched as that Corrigan story, well, let me get a few sacks of salt."

"Bryan, I'm serious."

"Okay. I'm listening. What?"

"I think I'm in love with Jeremy."

"Would you repeat that."

"I said I think I'm in love with Jeremy."

"Kevin, I think there must be something wrong with the water in California . . ."

"Listen, Bryan. I'm very serious. This time it's for real. I've even considered the possibility of moving here, I mean staying here, well, I mean I'd have to come back to New York to settle things, but well, I think I want to live here. With Jeremy."

"Have you discussed this with him?"

"Not exactly."

"Well, if I were you, I'd discuss it with Jeremy before you do anything rash. And what about your job?"

"I'll find another one."

"And the apartment?"

"It's yours. You can have Billy move in with you — if you think you're ready for a commitment — or you can keep it for yourself."

Bryan faked an exaggerated gasp. "You mean, you'd sign the lease over to me?"

"Yes."

"Do you mean it?"

"Yes, Bryan, I mean it."

"Of course, I'll miss you, but hey, this is great, it'll work out for the best all the way around . . . that is, if this Jeremy feels as strongly about you as you seem to feel about him."

"I've got to find out," said Kevin. "And there's only one way to do that. I've got to try or I'll never know for sure."

"When are you coming back?"

"Soon. I don't know yet. As soon as everything settles down a bit and I find out where I stand."

Chapter 21

The Church of Divine Forgiveness, usually so quiet and unassuming, looked like a supermarket at its gala opening. The peeling, weatherbeaten sign on the front door had been taken down and huge red banners proclaimed the importance of this institution. Klieg lights criss-crossed the night sky above, as though the Lord himself would make a special guest appearance. The TV ad campaign and the flyers that had been circulated attracted a sprawling crowd. People streamed into the open doors and when the interior was full, a huge throng blocked the entrance like a bottle stopper. Television technicians with harried faces pleaded with the milling crowd to please avoid the cables that ran through the doorway, down the steps, and into the mobile unit.

Within the faded, dusty walls, all seats had been claimed. About fifty people stood elbow to elbow in the rear between the last pew and the back wall. An ambulance tore down the street just outside, and the siren's whine entered the room like a spear, slicing the conversational drone in half. After a brief lull in the din, it grew back to full size.

In the anteroom backstage, the principals mingled. Reverend Bates paced back and forth, rubbing his hands together. Rosemary sat on the couch blowing her nose into a pink hanky. Billy stood still, so as not to soil or crease his white gown. Jack Corrigan sat on the couch, as far from Rosemary as the couch would allow. Aware that he was avoiding her, Rosemary moved to his side and whispered, "I need some more stuff. I'm sick as a dog and the last stuff you sold me didn't work."

"Not now," he urged. "I can't think about that now. Later."

Rosemary knew that he'd burned her and she'd not only lost the money, but would have to look for another source. This pained her. She grimaced as she moved back to the other end of the couch.

The Reverend observed their brief exchange but did not let on that he'd seen. He knew that his wife and his boss had

118

been conspiring behind his back, but he never imagined that they might be having an affair. The whispered conversation confirmed this. As soon as the taping was done he would inform Corrigan to keep his hands off his wife. And he'd punish her severely for her misdeeds.

Dan Greenburg entered, beaming like a soon-to-be proud father. He greeted everyone in the room except for Corrigan, whom he'd not met. Billy saw Greenburg hesitate when his eyes found Corrigan, so he took it upon himself to introduce them.

"Mr. Greenburg, this is Mr. Corrigan. Mr. Corrigan, this is Mr. Greenburg."

The two men shook hands, then Greenburg moved quickly to the Reverend's side. "Where's Tom Slater?"

The Reverend avoided looking at the empty green armchair. Forcing a reassuring smile he said, "He's upstairs. Won't be down until it's time."

"Okay," said Greenburg, offering an upraised thumb.

The taping was to begin at 6:30 but it was already 6:45. The people out front were impatient and restless.

Sitting in the third pew from the front, a few seats to the right of the center aisle, sat Leona Ramirez and Paulette Bluefeather. They were dressed in their formal best and sat with their hands in their laps, quietly awaiting the beginning of the church service. Sergeant Bolkonsky had telephoned earlier in the day and asked Leona if she'd ever heard of the Church of Divine Forgiveness.

"No, I haven't," she'd replied, curious about this question and excited by the sound of the Sergeant's voice.

He explained. "We have reason to believe Corrigan is channeling illegal funds through the church books. I thought maybe there was a connection with your husband's disappearance."

"I'm sorry, Sergeant, but I never heard of it."

"Then you've never been there?"

"No."

"Do you think you could be there tonight, at around 6:00? There's going to be a television taping and we suspect that Corrigan and his people will be there. Maybe you'll see someone you recognize, maybe you'll remember something."

She told him she'd be there, and when she'd informed Paulette of her intention to go, Paulette had insisted on accompanying her.

119

"It might be dangerous," she'd explained. "You shouldn't go alone." Paulette sat, staring straight ahead, wondering what all of this excitement was for. She believed that church services, like sexual intercourse, were not intended for broadcast purposes.

Leona tried to remain calm, but she was overwrought. Glancing around, she saw Kurt and Sam sitting in a pew across the aisle. Fortunately they hadn't spotted her. She wondered where Suzie could be. She must have been released from the closet by now.

Her thoughts turned to the decor. She compared the grungy walls and fake stained glass windows of the Church of Divine Forgiveness with the immaculate, well cared for appearance of the Church of St. Miguel. She was glad that she worshiped at St. Miguel's and hoped that she'd never have to come back to this place again. She arched her neck and looked at the candelabra above. It looked like a wagon wheel with candles perched on the rim. Unusual for a church, she thought. But then everything about this place was odd to her; it was unlike any other church she'd ever attended.

Standing in the back of the chapel, Sergeant Bolkonsky looked like a college student. In his uniform he looked older, authoritative. But in a button-down shirt and light blue sweater, the image was one of youthful innocence. His eyes casually swept the crowded room, searching for signs of disturbance, suspicious behavior. As soon as he'd entered, he'd noticed where Leona was seated. He felt very protective toward her, as though her dangerous position was his fault and he was responsible for her well-being. He had his gun in his pocket and patted it through the khaki pants material. Glancing at his wristwatch, he wondered when this circus was going to begin.

In a pew toward the rear, on the left-hand side, sat Thad, Weslya, Jeremy, and Kevin. They had smoked some of Weslya's special stuff before entering and were smashed. They whispered jokes to one another and played telephone — with Kevin or Thad whispering messages to pass along. The distortions were hysterical. They giggled and cupped their mouths, trying to squelch their laughter.

Standing just inside the doors of the church was Vince Pileggi. He had a small notepad and pen ready to write down anything that might contribute to his article on the taping or his investigation of the Corrigan empire. After reading all of the data his researchers had amassed, and comparing it with the information that Thad and Kevin had told him, he'd become convinced of Corrigan's guilt. It would do the world some good to expose him. And it wouldn't hurt Pileggi's burgeoning reputation as a crusader-in-print either.

Outside the church, on the steps, stood Drexel Johnson and Erika Hong. In their unyielding effort to sweep the city of arson, they'd discovered that a certain car registered to Jack Corrigan had been parked at the scene of the fire at the motel on Market Street. A computer search had revealed that the same car had been in the vicinity of two other suspicious fires, one about two months prior, the other shortly before that. Now the same car, which they'd been following for about a week, was parked just outside the church. They figured it would be wise to hang around and keep their eyes open.

Inside the church, the spotlights set up by the technical crew showered the stage with thick beams of brightness. The congregation hushed and a perfectly tanned announcer in a blue blazer and dark gray slacks approached the microphone at the apron of the stage.

"Ladies and gentlemen, good evening. Welcome to the first program taped at the Church of Divine Forgiveness before a live audience. We hope you will enjoy the show and just want to remind you that we're looking for lots of audience participation. So if you feel moved to cry, laugh, shout out 'Hallelujah!' don't hold back. Let it all hang out. We're here to put on a good show and have a good time. So relax and enjoy yourselves."

"I thought this was supposed to be live. What are they taping it for?" said Kurt to Sam.

Scattered applause greeted the announcer's speech. Then, through the church sound system, came the roll of kettle drums. The announcer looked straight into the camera to the left of the stage and said, "And now, live from the Church of Divine Forgiveness, we bring you the *Family Holy Hour* starring Reverend Lawrence Bates, featuring the lovely Rosemary Bates, the adorable Billy Bates and our special bonus attraction, the legendary Tom Slater!"

Sam said to Kurt, "It *is* gonna be on tape. They want the people at home to *think* it's live."

"Oh."

The audience rose, cheering, whistling, and clapping as the Reverend came from behind the black drapes. With his arms raised and his jaw set, he strode to the podium and pounded it with his fist. "My fellow sinners!" he shouted, the veins in his neck standing out like taut ropes. "What are you willing to give for divine forgiveness? Your heart? Your soul? Your cash? Your blood?"

As the applause died down, the congregation settled. Eerie organ music dripped from the speakers as the Reverend expounded on faith, charity, and the Holy Spirit.

Paulette leaned over to Leona and whispered, "The phoney-baloney." Thad draped his arm along the back of the pew behind Weslya's head. Jeremy and Kevin held hands and did their best not to laugh out loud. Dan Greenburg knelt by the side of the stage.

A groaning sound suddenly permeated the chapel. Followed by a loud smack. It sounded like it came from above. Several heads looked up at the ceiling. The Reverend glanced up but didn't miss a syllable. A moment after the sounds had faded, a sharp splintering interrupted the proceedings.

A voice rang out from somewhere, "The candles! Watch out below!"

The candelabra plummeted, crashing into the heads and shoulders of the unfortunates beneath. People screamed and shot to their feet, pushing others out of the way, heading for the doors. Several candles fell off the broken wheel and rolled on the floor. A woman's dress caught fire. She screeched and started whirling around, tears streaming down her panic-stricken face. As the flames engulfed the dress, several people moved away from her. A couple tried to help her but she wouldn't stand still and couldn't be subdued.

The people outside didn't know what was happening. The doors were blocked and no one could get out. The aisles were jammed with bodies pushing and shoving but none could advance.

In the melee, Thad got separated from Weslya, Kevin lost Jeremy and Paulette couldn't find Leona. With pounding hearts and smoke-teared eyes, they were torn between locating their companions and trying to escape. Flames were climbing the walls and people who'd lost their balance and fallen were crushed beneath the raging crowd.

Sergeant Bolkonsky managed to push his way to the doors. He flung people aside and dragged arms and waists to clear an opening. Finally, people trapped inside were able to exit. The sergeant controlled the traffic at the door as the congregation stampeded toward safety.

As smoke billowed into the sky and fire danced on the curtains by the open windows above the chapel, Kurt and Sam exited and ran toward the car parked at the curb. As they opened the doors and readied themselves to get inside, Drexel and Erika confronted them. While Drexel had called the station to report the fire, Erika kept an eye on Corrigan's car while assisting some elderly folks who'd just managed to escape.

"Hey, buddy," said Drexel, grabbing Sam's arm, "what's your hurry?"

"Yeah," said Erika, "you going to a fire or something?"

They pulled summonses from their pockets, handed one to a bewildered Kurt and the other to a scowling Sam.

"What's this?" Sam growled.

"Read it and weep, firebug," said Drexel.

"See you in court," said Erika.

As the firetrucks roared onto the street and the firemen started unrolling the hoses, Sergeant Bolkonsky oversaw the rescue operation. There were still people inside who had to be gotten out. He grabbed hold of a man who was screaming, flailing his arms. He slapped his face, pulled his arms down, and half-pushed him to the door.

The sound of crashing timber and crackling flames could be heard above the shouts from human throats. Weslya emerged, coughing and choking. Bolkonsky put his arm around her waist and helped her down the stairs. Suddenly the water came on and giant tongues of quicksilver licked the outside of the building. A moment later, Leona stumbled out the door, her eyes watering, as she supported Dan Greenburg, who'd almost succumbed to asphyxiation. She helped him to the sidewalk where he sat, shaking, fighting for air.

When the police arrived to help, they moved the people on the steps away from the building. Just as most of the crowd was out of the way, a loud snap reverberated as the roof of the church caved in. As shards and cinders shot into the sky, a side wall collapsed, followed almost immediately by its opposite. Smoke and flames feathered into the dark sky as the rubble of what had once been a church became soaked with precious water.

A few hours later, all of the people had gone home. A few embers still glowed and occasional wisps of smoke drifted from the wet debris. It took all night, however, to recover all the bodies.

Chapter 22

The burning of the church affected some people who had never seen it. Like the aftershocks of an earthquake, this event continued to bring tremors to certain lives long after the actual flames had drowned. People are linked by invisible network lines. There is very little of consequence that does not ultimately influence many fates. Had the church not been destroyed, would the future have been different? Most likely. And what event in the past had caused the candelabra to detach from the ceiling beams? Could an earthquake have loosened the fastening screws? Or perhaps the timber had become soaked with Tom and Suzie's blood, causing the wood to loosen its grip? Maybe it was something that nobody could ever imagine.

The charred ruins of the church languished for several months. After the corpses had been reclaimed and identified; after the insurance claims and real estate legalities had been surmounted; after the money had been gathered and apportioned, the site was cleared and a new building erected on the lot. A facsimile of its predecessor, it was styled in Neo-Victorian trappings on the outside but the interior was stylishly contemporary.

The first floor was divided into two gallery spaces — one for Native American crafts, the other for modern paintings and prints. On the second floor were two apartments with a shared kitchen. Paulette Bluefeather and Billy Bates, now her adopted son, lived above the crafts gallery. Kevin Conover and Jeremy Willis occupied the other apartment, over the art gallery. The attic on the third floor was devoted mainly to storage space with both living units having equal access. Across from all the stacked cartons and luggage, Jeremy built himself a small office in which he installed a desk and chair, typewriter, bookshelf, and gooseneck lamp.

It was a pleasant afternoon on a sunny weekday and, for a change, business was slow at both galleries. Paulette scanned a magazine in the crafts shop. Jeremy, filling in for Kevin, stared out the window. Eventually, he wanted to stretch his legs, so he rose and stepped into the next room. Paulette looked up.

"Greetings, stranger," she smiled. Her hair was like an obsidian waterfall on her shoulders. She wore a fringed buckskin caftan.

"Kind of slow today, huh?" he asked.

Paulette took in his lithe form, well-defined in tight jeans and a tank top. His eyes looked a little weary, though. Probably from staring at all that small print. Born in another place and time, he might have been a shaman. "How goes the book?"

"It goes very slowly," he replied. "You know how it is."

She nodded in agreement. "And where's Kevin today?"

"Picking up the last of his parcels from New York. It's taken a long time for him to finally get his life back together into one piece."

"Ah, I know what you mean," she said.

Jeremy knew she was referring to Billy. He asked how he was doing. "Better. It's going to take a while but I can see very gradual improvement. He's adjusting to school faster than I thought he would. But he misses his parents so much I can barely compensate."

"It's been tough on the kid. But I think he's a survivor for sure." Paulette nodded again and asked Jeremy if he'd like a mug of tea. "Love some."

Paulette, Kevin, and Jeremy split the mortgage and upkeep payments on the entire building. It took some time for Kevin's gallery to attract attention from the critical establishment; many of his artists were East Coast based and had not yet become accepted nationally. Fortunately he had enough money saved to get through those first months. Then business picked up and continued to grow at an impressive rate.

Paulette had achieved instant success. Her boutique was the first of its kind and became very popular right away with natives and tourists. Blankets, rugs, pottery, weavings, paintings, and folk sculpture adorned the walls and glass cases of her shop and the customers were lavish with their effusive praise and free with their money.

After Jeremy abandoned the autobiography he'd started, he began researching the life of Jack Corrigan. He submitted an outline and query to a publisher who eventually invited him out to lunch. After a lengthy discussion, Jeremy shook his hand and subsequently signed a two-book contract. The first would be a biography of Jack Corrigan. The second would be the autobiography of Jeremy Willis.

☆ ☆ ☆

For almost nine months, Kurt and Sam served time in prison for conspiracy, fraud, arson, and complicity. The sentence had been from three to ten years, but they got time off for good behavior and the promise that they'd work in a community services program.

They became the core of a Fire Department Squad formed to prevent incendiary situations — under the supervision of Drexel Johnson and Erika Hong.

In the basement of an abandoned building in the Tenderloin, Drexel and Erika held flashlights while Kurt and Sam, ankle-deep in debris, collected flammable rags, planks, paint cans, and cushions.

"I hate this fuckin' shit," said Kurt under his breath.

"Pipe down," said Sam, sweeping his hair from his forehead, leaving a streak of grease, "or those two bulldykes will hear us and . . ."

"Those two what?" asked Drexel, her voice rising in anticipation.

"You don't think they'd refer to us as *dykes*," smirked Erika. "Would you, boys?"

"No, ma'am," said Kurt.

"You'll never hear us complain," Sam quickly added. He looked up and grinned.

"Well, that's sure a relief," chuckled Erika, shining the flashlight in Sam's eyes. "We'd just *hate* to have to put you guys on report. They might send you back to prison for — oh, I don't know — three or four years and frankly, I don't think your delicate butts could handle it. Drexel?"

"Nah. These guys are too *refined* for prison life. I think they're going to be good little boys because, Erika, darlin', I'd be just as mad at myself as you would be at yourself if we had to send these two *aristocrats* back to *Sodomyville*."

Erika started to laugh. Drexel joined her. Soon they were howling with mirth. Sam and Kurt looked away and continued filling barrels with hazardous junk.

☆ ☆ ☆

Once the cops and reporters had gotten on his case, Jack Corrigan was as vulnerable as an exposed nerve. Thanks to the testimony of Kurt and Sam, he was convicted of murder, conspiracy, fraud, and complicity. His lawyer attempted to have his behavior excused on the grounds that he was alcoholic and therefore, mentally unfit and not responsible for his actions. The jury did not buy this for one second. And after the overwhelming testimony provided by Leona, Thad, Kevin, Weslya, Kurt, and Sam, he was sentenced to life imprisonment with no parole.

At first, jail seemed almost like a relief to him. He had no responsibilities to fulfill, no projects to complete, no money to collect. It was a respite from the maelstrom of mental activity and stress overload that had enabled him to build his empire. It seemed that he'd always had to burn his synapses to make his plans work and now he could simply relax and not worry about anything.

But he was unused to the austere life of penal institutions. He hated having to wash, eat, and live with blacks, Chicanos, Asians, some of whom were homosexual. But most of all, he didn't like being told what to do. Used to being his own boss and doing as he pleased, he resisted the efforts of the guards, block leaders, and warden to break his spirit and make him grovel.

When he could no longer tolerate his situation, he plotted to end his misery. He bribed a guard with one of several large bills he'd smuggled into the prison. The guard supplied him with a vial of pain killers and a fork from the cafeteria. Late one night, after the lights were out and everyone was asleep, Corrigan swallowed all of the pills. Then before dozing off, he opened the veins of his wrists with the dull tines of the fork.

His body was discovered early the next morning. Blood had puddled beneath his bed, then flowed in rivulets under the lowest bars of the cell into the hallway of lifer's row.

The guard who'd supplied Corrigan with the tranquilizers and the weapon arranged to discover the body. The first thing he did was search Corrigan's cell and body. When he found the rest of Corrigan's money, tucked up in his forbidden zone, he hid the bills in his shoe and then reported the suicide to the warden.

No one claimed Corrigan's body. He was buried in the prison cemetery after a brief and solemn eulogy from Father Ernesto, the prison pastor.

☆ ☆ ☆

In the shifting and settling that occurred after the fire and Corrigan's suicide, Weslya and Andrew Bolkonsky bought

Paulette Bluefeather's small white house and moved in together right after their wedding.

A small civil ceremony, it was held about six months after they met. They'd started dating. Andrew had fallen in love with her kind and gentle face, her lean and supple body when he'd held her in his arms on the steps of the burning church. Weslya was so grateful for his solicitude and assistance, she felt indebted. But this sense of obligation soon gave way to a genuine admiration for this man who was so caring, so organized, so, well, together.

Weslya threw herself into housewifery and motherhood. She redecorated the small house. Weathered planks and oil lamps, shaggy rugs and western prints dominated the interior. Outside, the house looked the same, but with a new coat of white paint. Weslya planted a small garden in the backyard. But her main priority was to have children and she happily announced to Andrew, shortly after their honeymoon in Hawaii, that she was pregnant. Andrew was thrilled and had some good news for her a few weeks after that — he'd been promoted to lieutenant.

Pregnant, Weslya filled out nicely. Her breasts ripened and her hips became rounder. She started wearing looser clothing and her face looked more serene, her skin became opalescent.

In the evenings, after Andrew got home, Weslya would cook a vegetarian meal. When he wanted meat, he had it for lunch, usually at a restaurant with a fellow officer. Weslya was partial to whole grains, beans, vegetables, pasta, fruit, and homemade breads. Andrew had always been a burger-and-fries kind of guy, but he grew to love her apple butter and seven-grain bread, pinto-broccoli casserole, fettucini primavera, and rhubarb pie. They drank mu tea with dinner, but Andrew drank coffee all day at work.

After dinner, they'd sit in the living room. Weslya knitted hats, gloves, scarves, and sweaters for the coming child. Andrew read, alternating between adventure stories, child care manuals, and nature studies. Sometimes Weslya would smoke a joint and play music on their stereo while she knitted. Andrew never smoked anything or drank any alcohol. But there was no friction resulting from this division of preference.

☆ ☆ ☆

Although she wasn't ready to marry him yet, Leona finally agreed to move into Dan Greenburg's apartment on the thirty-third floor of an ultra-modern co-op. It was a floor-sized unit with wrap-around windows overlooking the ocean, bay, and in the distance, Mount Tamalpais.

After it became evident that Greenburg would have to find a replacement for the *Family Holy Hour*, he spent a great deal of time trying to figure out what kind of programming would increase the station's viewership and thereby, reflect favorably on his hard work and keen vision. He'd met Leona during the panic within the burning church and he'd been immediately struck by her beauty; the dark, brooding eyes, the full, inviting lips, the burnished, coppery skin. At first, his interest in her was purely physical. But once he got to know her and learned how intelligent and concerned she was, it occurred to him that the future of local television broadcasting might be tied up with local ethnic communities. He took her out several times and discussed the possibility of Leona becoming his liaison to the Chicano community.

At first, Leona didn't trust him. But she liked the idea of serving her community as a media consultant. And once she got to know him better, she realized that Dan Greenburg was basically a good man. A bit too ambitious, perhaps, but like herself, once he'd established a goal for himself he couldn't rest until it was attained.

It had begun with a few dinners, an occasional concert or play. By that time Greenburg was hooked and wanted Leona all to himself all of the time. He asked her if she'd marry him. She wondered if Enrique would approve. After realizing that she'd never know, she refused the offer of marriage but suggested the possibility of living together. Dan agreed right away.

Leona moved out of Paula's home, right before it was sold to Weslya and Andrew. At first she didn't like Dan's apartment. It seemed too antiseptic and high-toned. So she added her own personal touches; new brightly colored drapes instead of the unimaginative white ones, some paintings and sculptures she purchased at Paula's gallery, a stereo system with speakers and controls in every room of the apartment.

While Dan spent his days at the office, Leona divided her time between her television responsibilities and her position as co-executor of Jack Corrigan's estate. She and Thad Heath had been appointed to jointly sort out Corrigan's financial holdings, try to reimburse those who'd been robbed, and channel funds into community services. Leona met with Thad twice a week. It took almost a year to figure out what belonged to whom and then twice that length of time to contact Corrigan's victims. Some were never found, but the rest were very grateful.

☆ ☆ ☆

"This magazine smells like a French whore's bedsheets," said Thad. He wrinkled his nose in disgust and tossed the magazine onto the coffee table. He hated stylishly fashionable magazines and he hated cloyingly sweet scents. Cologne ads in print were his latest pet peeve. Thad was with Weslya and Kevin, in Kevin and Jeremy's apartment above the art gallery. The walls and ceiling were painted gray with a violet trim. The decor was a combination of butcher block surfaces, deco fixtures, and abstract paintings. Kevin and his guests sat on a sectional sofa which made an L around a glass table on driftwood legs.

"Yeah," said Kevin, "what's the world coming to when you can't read a magazine without throwing up."

Weslya smiled. She welcomed the meetings between herself, Thad, and Kevin. They'd been like a team during their dealings with Corrigan and his gang. Every time they got together it was like a spirited reunion. Jeremy was upstairs typing. Andrew was at a Police Athletic League meeting, and Thad was bored. So he'd called Weslya and Kevin and arranged this meeting. The three of them sat, sipping wine coolers, talking aimlessly.

"How's the sax coming?" Kevin asked.

"And your poetry," added Weslya.

"As long as I don't forget that it ain't 1958 any more, everything's fine." Thad had decided to devote himself to learning to play the tenor saxophone and writing poems. In 1969, after his honorable discharge from Vietnam, he'd stumbled upon an album, recorded in 1958, of poets reading their work as jazz musicians improvised in the background. He'd toyed with the idea of learning to play and write, but hadn't done anything about it until recently. His goal was to make his own recordings of himself reading his poems, playing sax in support. He'd bought himself a home eight-track recording unit and spent a lot of time exploring the possibilities. Sometimes he'd read a written poem and overdub an improvised accompaniment. Sometimes he'd play a composed piece and improvise a spontaneous poem on top of that. Sometimes he'd blend a composed poem with a composed piece of music or he'd improvise both. His goal was to study and document these four methods until he'd accumulated a backlog of good recordings in which he could take pride.

Thad sipped and looked at Weslya, so peaceful and content. He'd almost developed a crush on her, but soon enough realized that he admired her more than he loved her.

"Well," said Weslya, "what's next? Life is dull without a caper."

"I don't know," said Thad, "I want to take care of some personal business for now. When something happens that we should do something about, we'll know it."

"I know it sounds like I'm asking for trouble," said Kevin, "but I would welcome another opportunity to pounce on some asshole and give him what he's got coming."

"That's the spirit," said Weslya.

Just then, Thad glanced at his wristwatch. "Shit! I'm supposed to call Lydia. I almost forgot. Kevin, may I use the phone?"

"Of course."

Thad went to the bedroom to speak in private.

As soon as he was gone, Weslya whispered, "Who's Lydia?"

"He's been dating her for almost two months. I haven't met her yet but I think he's really serious."

"Why hasn't he told me about her?"

"I really don't know, Wes. Maybe he doesn't want to talk about it because it's bad luck. The only reason he told me is because I flat out asked him if he was seeing anyone."

Weslya tried not to look petulant. "How's Jeremy?" she asked, concerned about his welfare, now that she'd forgiven him.

"Great. Writing like a maniac. How's Andy?"

"The best. He's always in a good mood so I'm always in a good mood."

"That's great."

For a few moments neither could think of anything to say.

"You seem bored," said Weslya.

"No. It's just everything's been so quiet lately. Nothing very exciting to speak of . . . you haven't touched the wine," he said.

Weslya patted her rounded belly. "Goin' easy these days."

"I suppose you don't have any smoke?"

"I've got some," she said languidly, "but I don't want to smoke any. You can, though." She reached for the burlap shoulder bag on the floor and felt around inside, then pulled out a

131

thin joint and tossed it on the table. "Here. Enjoy it for all three of us." She grinned and patted her belly again.

"I'll wait for Thad."

Weslya smiled. "I've been meaning to ask you — now that you're settled and everything — do you miss New York?"

Kevin ran his fingers through his hair and sighed. "Sometimes. There's more energy there. But it's prettier here. And I can always go back to visit any time I want to. I love it here. There's no place else in the entire universe like San Francisco."

Weslya nodded in agreement.

Suddenly, they felt a tremor beneath their feet.